BOMBAY CITY OF SANDALS

BOMBAY
CITY OF SANDALS

Shänne Sands

UNITED WRITERS
Cornwall

UNITED WRITERS PUBLICATIONS LTD
Trevail Mill, Zennor, St. Ives, Cornwall.

ISBN 901976 72 5

Printed in Great Britain by
United Writers Publications Ltd
Cornwall

To My Precious Son

Daniel.H. --

My Bringer of Happiness

CONTENTS

FAIR BAY

Bombay is a hot, sensual city, where everything and everyone moves in time to the swaying palm-trees. Endless crowds drift through the hot, dusty streets from dawn till sudden darkness for no twilight softens the abrupt ending to an eastern day. A huge burning sun's heat breaks across their backs warming at the same moment dozens of mangy cats, millions of over-fed, over-noisy crows, green parrots, tiny sparrows that seem strangely out of place in an eastern city. Untold variety of tropical birds adorned in lovely exotic feathers and packs of hungry, unloved dogs even more mangy and rabid than the cats.

Insects that outnumber all other living creatures fly or creep or bite or sting. Buzz and hum over pavements, along marble floors, up and down walls, drift on silky threads across ceilings and dangle from big, black electric fans that look like monsters all twisted with cobwebs as they twirl out warm, windy air from spicy smelling rooms.

With the inevitable sacred cows pushing for their honoured place along the roadside near a not so holy buffalo cart. Stray chickens enjoy a brief escape from a wicker-basket left un-attended for a moment in a back street bazaar. They pick at sacred droppings while squirrels with a touch of England about them, run up and down the trees keeping time to the rather mournful sound of bleating goats, whose tormentors, flies and ants are everywhere.

Fair Bay or Great Mother, Maha Amma is known the world over as Bombay. Like most Indian cities she is a difficult Great Mother, churning the emotions. Quick to anger, quick to love, quick to tears, even quicker for the dying. Saris twirl past the old, narrow streets. Streets alive with cockroaches and huge black rats that procreate themselves almost as fast as the swarming flies around the heaps of stale dung, left in odd corners.

High in the trees the bright green parrots cackle a kind of tormented song. The sun with its cruel power, becomes a dictator burning the body and each day except for the monsoon weather is a copy of the day before. Hot. Flame hot. Hot. Flame Hot. Until the sun leaves the sky falling abruptly into an overheated sea.

Millions of insects humming and ugly bite into the warm flesh as you sleep. You become a sun-drenched idiot always damp with sweat. Unable to forget the heat you play with the air-conditioner's switches and drink like a bibacious fool, cursing the tropical city, where heat and dirt and too much humanity separate you from any kind of charity towards the poverty.

One beggar becomes the same as another beggar. One hungry child just another poor Indian to look at taking your pick from millions, feel hopeless about their lives, shudder at the sores and filth, curse the state of undeveloped, backward countries and then pass on and yet again on, leaving perhaps a few small coins of little value in a brown-soiled palm.

The poverty-stricken dark-skinned ones cannot escape from the wheel of incarnations, cannot go back far into ages lost and forgotten. Back into the security of the ancient forests they left in other lives so long ago.

Back to the warmth of their sacred fires to dance their dance of existence before Lord Krishna and ask to be lifted from the gutters. To raise their beautiful eyes to a hopeful sky. Not to be poor and desireless with Hindu pessimism, but to be filled with certain desires. A certain joy that life was meant to be a richer experience than to beg at the foot of another Indian who simply places a beggar's fate in the lap of one of a thousand gods or one of a thousand Castes.

But I will try to wake the gods up. Shout their names for sound is pleasing to them. I will ring my bells till their ears ache. I will cry to Siva the great god who is Lord and Master of asceticism, who wears the Brahman cord and whose forehead is often marked by three horizontal stripes with a third eye staring from its centre. I will cry to him to come with me. Also to Parvati the daughter of the Himalayas and Siva's gracious, brilliant, but sometimes inaccessible goddess wife. A feminine divinity of Hindu power. I will cry to Brahma to turn from stone. He who is the creative god, the father of all gods and men, shall leap from his temple and Vishnu asleep on the snake Anant-Sesha will wake, arise before dawn, wash their feet and come through the streets. To see the sleeping poor and the fresh born waking to a day of nothingness. To listen and hear the Cries of India coming down the centuries, touching Buddha's mouth at the corners as he smiles softly at all these people waking to the chant of an old, bent beggar man.

Forgetting for a second the large important houses that glitter white against the blue sky. Forgetting the busy offices and opulent apartment blocks that tower above the heads of the poor. Forgetting that poverty is a supposed natural law hardly cared about or maybe not even noticed by most Indians and foreigners, who accept suffering, because India is such a 'poor country', left desolate by too many invaders. Forgetting all the words and schemes and lost ideals. Dead political giants and glorious Hindu saints. Forgetting even the corrupt grain merchants and dreaded money-lenders from the Bania caste who come from desert cities in Rajasthan to become successful merchants in Bombay. All hiding behind the backs of obese, white trousered blackmarketeers!

Forget for a moment you lazy gods this city of commerce, wealth and honour; this city of history and horror and come with me through the streets of Old Mumbai.

Gods smother your demons. Eat them up and walk along the roadside to where a patch of red soil throws up bright scarlet gladioli as red as chilli-pepper. As red as the blood of the hungry, as red as their anger. Do not be misled by the soft look in the dark brown eyes. The poor are angry, hungry and dying.

Come gods everyone loves Bombay and calls her with affection 'Old Mumbai'. Again and again they return to wander through the heartless city. For though the Great Mother never refuses sanctuary to any of the endless thousands of bare feet that tread her hot pavements, she is a harsh mistress for those who have no money. I will cry to the gods to look high into the Banyan trees. No rupees grow there for the poor to gather from sheltering branches. Only half-ripened figs are their harvest. They curl up underneath these thick, spreading trees and sleep the sleep of those who have little to be active for and perhaps they dream or lie listless in groups, wondering where they can go when the monsoon breaks upon their ragged bodies.

It was an old 17th-century proverb, a time in her history when the Great Mother was still only a wilderness of malarious mud-flats and dense coconut plantations, that 'two monsoons' are the life of a man. Even today a beggar child can be oddly blessed to see one monsoon. But it is not yet time for the rainy season of Varsha. The rains have not wetted the red earth. The streets are hot. Bombay is alive with a living mass of people.

A tropical roundabout. An ancient civilisation making a human coloured dragon of Castes and creeds and races moving like a never ending television spectacular across the city. While the Arabian sea laps at its edges like a thirsty puppy maybe waiting to take back the land that was reclaimed from its muddy swamps long ago!

DIWALI - THE BEGINNING

In the beginning there was darkness and God said, 'Let there be light, and lo! There was light.

In bombay there was darkness after the sun's departure from its blue-hot heavens and the people said, 'Let there be Diwali' and lo! On the new moon of Kartik, which is the season of Autumn, the lamps were aflame and lights, millions of pretty lights, from every window, every shop, every corner of the city shone into the night air.

Flickering beams from candles and light bulbs across the hearts of the people.

Diwali, Festival of Lights and Hindu New-Year. Feast of Lamps. A scene as lovely as the new-moon that brings the festival to life. As lovely as the Goddess Lakshmi who is honoured with the dancing lamps placed by an adoring city at her feet.

She will bring even more prosperity to the merchants and bankers who count their wealth and worship its meaning before the Lakshmi shrines. Their treasures are lit-up before their eyes by so many bright candles. For this is the day Vishnu, God dressed in yellow against the dark blue of his skin and riding an eagle, becomes the light of the whole universe and with three steps, he crossed the world, penetrating it with light. This is the day Vishnu killed a giant and Hindu women go out with lighted lamps to meet him and his wife the goddess Lakshmi, born from the churning sea, perfumed and confident of Vishnu's love, brings her gifts of light and adds them to the lighted lamps of the city. This is the night of feasting and laughter.

The beginning, the prayers from the people to the gods

for rice. The chant of the mothers for fertility. The beginning of thanks to Vishnu, eternal light of the sun.

'Here we are, gods of our fathers and we bring you lamps and as we caste them on rivers, set them afloat in the warm sea, what auguries will be drawn from them. What floating messages of hope or doom will fade into the rushing waters?'

And the gods asked for sound, for they are greedy gods. Light was not enough. They wanted big, enormous sound and the people made a tremendous noise banging their drums and dancing through the streets and along the sands till their heels blistered and they gave their gods fireworks. Letting them off days before Diwali and the city became a huge, colourful bang of innocence.

Lights and sounds, flame and noise, it is the beginning. The people are free to dance and crayon their welcome patterns in front of door-ways and up flights of stairs. Candles burn. Light up your houses. Let off fireworks from the tops of your flat-roofed mansions. A lone coconut-wallah* boy gazed in silent wonder at the sprays of falling cinders. He is too poor to have any fireworks of his own, but adds the pure light in his brown eyes to those around him. Let the gods see the city; the faces of the people reflected in the bright mirror of light.

Light up your skies for this is the beginning. Diwali shall raise the roof off the sky and fireworks shall replace the stars.

Morning has broken with a fresh dawn and a mild wind, soft and warm helps the red and white sailed fishing dhows into Bombay harbour. The palm trees sway the cawing crows to life and the night of fireworks had ended for another year. There is not a flash of light to be seen or any lamps left floating on the waters. All is quiet. Only the birds make it known that the city is about to wake-up, before the sun becomes a vicious, burning lump of fire.

Driving from the suburbs just after seven in the morning I watched the street scenes move from solitude into the rush of another day. Shop-keepers brushing their teeth outside the shaky doors of their shack-dwellings, where they live and work. No tube of toothpaste for them, but a white powder called monkey-powder. Using a brass pot filled with water drawn from a water-pump in the middle of the side

* Wallah — English equivalent to 'Fellow'

road, making all the coughs and splutters and spits of advance
'flu, as one finger dark and slender rubs the monkey-powder
up and down and side-ways and across the huge, gleaming
white teeth. While at the same water-pump women splash
water over their naked children. Secure the sacred black
thread around the children's bottoms, worn to show their
Hindu sect and to keep off the evil eye. They rub coconut
oil through their hair and with long, lean arms they pound
at the daily washing. Banging it against the stones. Stretch-
ing high as if to reach the gods. Their saris woven of homespun khaddi village cloth are tied above their knees and
the first early morning rays of sunlight gleam on their jet
black strands of hair.

The children splash in the morning cool as mongrel dogs
scratch and snarl at each other. An odd looking spider
monkey hangs from a tree and almost the whole street population have urinated, squatting up against walls, already
scarred bright scarlet with constant pan-spitting. Public-
conveniences are unheard of in India and the people lack all
inhibition about such earthy deeds as scratching, spitting
and urinating underneath their blue, blue skies.

The ayahs have by now hung the mornings washing out to
dry. From the balconies of smart flats and from windows of
old houses, from almost every available window in sight the
garments blow in the fresh breeze. Saris and bright cotton
towels, dhotis* and bed-sheets, childrens clothes and
brushed carpets and mats.

Soon they will iron the saris crumpled in the night of
fireworks, fun and flickering lamps. Many of the Great
Mother's huge population are not Hindu, yet they also let
off their share of Diwali firecrackers and saris become twisted
and torn and hundreds of pairs of neatly starched white
trousers have burn marks on the legs the next day.

Wearing strict white, the colour of Hindu mourning, old
women deep in widowhood, who long since have broken
their bangles in the last grief of marriage, at the deaths of
their husbands now make early morning offerings to their
favourite god or goddess. Young husbands and wives sip
spiced tea together before leaving for work, very much

*Dhoti — a length of white cotton fabric tied and worn below the male-
waist — traditional Hindu trousers.

15

like middle-class couples in other parts of the world.

Of course the idle, rich women are also there in enclosed splendour. Lovely, pampered, dark skinned dolls belonging to immensely wealthy families. They are idle, proud and slightly bored all their lives, but have a charm that lingers.

Servants wander around the houses and apartments beginning the day of cleaning, cooking and looking after the young. A glimmer of the ancients with their slaves is captured in the mind's eye. Nimble hands weave hair into long, black silky plaits. Girls from devout Hindu backgrounds are not allowed to cut their hair and plaits can be seen that touch the tip of a tanned heel. The older women make their buns glisten with slightly too much smelly coconut oil or even more exotic jasmine oil. Very old women swing to and fro on indoor swing couches and the old men sit quietly watching it all like proud old cats.

The Europeans who still have careers in the East, after the decline of white rule stretch golden limbs, leave a few instructions for the days routine with a willing servant, tell the cook what to buy in the markets and then leave the orderly flat or bungalow on Cumballa Hill or Napean Sea Road, to play a round of golf at their club, before they go to work in an air-conditioned English or American Company office. The Russians and Chinese are there too, just to keep an eye on things or so it seems!

On the pavements below a towering block of offices a mother sits in a forgotten corner beginning her day by killing the fleas taken from her child's hair. A million or so other mothers like her are performing the same act of skill and devotion and if a child is old enough to know how, it will in turn clean the mother's hair of lice and fleas.

Going through a dustbin a little boy finds an over-ripe banana and with a wry grin shares his find with his brother. Their mother stares into space, rubbing her belly, which sadly bulges with another baby soon to be born. The space in the road will soon be crowded with rushing business traffic breaking the speed limits in the morning haste to reach the centre of commerce.

In this city of millions, somehow it is the visual cameos I remember. The small child with a crippled leg. The blind man being led by a boy. The bare feet in a pool of water. The girl placing her wet saris, after washing them, on the grass to dry. The peasant with a basket of fruit on his head. The sleeping man huddled in a dirty loin-cloth outside a doorway leading to nowhere.

Near a taxi-rank some of the nights dead have been collected and a small mission sister, her pale face gazing at the thin corpses, makes the sign of the cross.

A buffalo cart rumbles past followed by a swarm of flies enough to spread the plague. No one takes any notice. The mystic beauty of a young girl in a pink sari and two young students laughing on their way to college with of all things a huge tropical dragon-fly buzzing around their heads.

A very British double-decker red bus packed with workers and the traffic control policeman with his navy shorts and comical thin legs standing on his perch in the centre of the road like a humanized bird using his hands and arms like wings. He looks as if he is about to fly away from it all.

The city in less than an hour will become a moving, shouting picture of sun and dust and endless people all gathered together by a kind of tropical madness.

The walking crowds seem afraid to be still for too long and they are caught and held in a glance for a second only, as the air with its smells of spice and dung moves the palms to an early morning ballet of bright green beauty.

Diwali has given a new beginning. Only the Grant Road prostitutes are asleep, all their energy spent. Bombay is strangely immutable. Her Westernising a mere hoax.

CASA DA VINCI

I came to the Great Mother as a young bride. For me those early days were days of discovery. Bombay was a giant kaleidoscope. Her coloured patterns falling into shape and order. I shook the fabric of my own beginnings within her days and nights and began the experience of Indian life with the excitement and longings of a girl of nineteen.

It was Spring, Vasanta in Hindi. The superconstellation I'd flown from London in made a perfect touch-down at Santa-Cruz airport ten miles from Bombay. I left the plane with my husband and the red soil of India was beneath my feet for the first time.

Vinci Wadia a member of one of the great society families of India, listed in the Encyclopaedia Britannica, as Ship Builders, was my first husband. The name Wadia means in Persian 'builder of ships'. A famous Parsi family to which Bombay owes a debt of thanks, because of its many philanthropic foundations that bear the Wadia name.

Wadia Movie-Tone my father-in-laws film company took the family into the world of the film industry and the very hectic life-style that goes with it. So my arrival in Bombay, as a bride of the Wadia's only son, was a little different to most travellers flying east.

The Air-India flight Captain knowing newly-weds were on board called Wadia took us into the cockpit, where champagne seemed to come 'out of the blue' and the crew offered us their greetings. I was even allowed to take over the controls for a few brief minutes, but was pretty sure it was George, the automatic pilot, that kept us all in flight.

For eight years my husband had been away from home.

The years of Public School and University in England. His parents had seldom seen him. Now he returned a handsome man with a British wife.

Photographers pushed to take pictures, his boyhood friends were standing in line to welcome him as the family draped garlands of flowers around our necks and placed coconuts in our hands for special luck and blessings. Then kisses and handshakes, before we all left in a rush of movement and laughter and much noise, driving in an eight-seater blue American Cadillac, heading away from Santa Cruz to their home in the suburbs of Bombay.

In the deep afternoon heat, as real, live chameleons lay stiff and still on blanched stones in a garden, where green lawns stretched towards the Arabian sea-front, as banana trees and palms entwined with plants of vivid tropical reds and oranges and faint specks of purple, swayed with sea breeze and just a slight touch of sea-spray wetted my face, I saw Casa da Vinci, the home of the Wadias, for the first time.

My very new mother-in-law was a romantic and had a special love of Italian architecture and Italian place names. Thus the house was of Italian design named after the city of Vinci, where my husband's name also came from. Perhaps rather eccentric in the midst of an Indian city, but it was built for a beautiful Persian woman, when she was a bride and of course it was a very fine house.

From its balconies and flat rooftops, as time passed by, I watched the tides of the Arabian waters come and go. I saw fresh dawns bring the days to life and sunsets turn the skies into a blaze of pinks. I stood underneath night skies and watched the stars till they made my eyes blink and I felt the Fair Bay enter into my mind, her music had begun to use my heart-strings to play a tune upon. I knew I would leave and return, leave and return, again and again. By sea, by air, the East had claimed part of my destiny. It was written on the sands a message for me to read as a horoscope or hand is read by a wise old Sikh.

Bombay the capital city of the State of Maharashtra, in the Indian Republic, seaport and home of the Wadias, had stolen a part of myself from me.

No part of my dowry had Bombay as a gift, that pleasure

was the birthright of Catherine of Braganza, when she married Charles II in 1661. But I fondled the square-cut ruby clustered with diamonds that my husband gave me. His mother had been given the same ring by her mother-in-law and now it was mine, matching in brilliance the bright red flowers in the garden and the twinkling stars in the night sky.

Garlands of white lilies hung from every doorway and archway in the house and the household servants from the cook to the smallest bathboy stood in the marble hall to say, 'Salam Memsahib'. Friends came from miles around to welcome us. The house was alive with people, people everywhere. But, I was very young. England and my own family were suddenly, thousands of miles across the seas that circled Bombay and like many a young girl before me who had left her home to live overseas, I wept. On my very first night in Casa da Vinci, in the bedroom, that had been so beautifully prepared for us, as the night lilies perfumed the air and my husband drew back the shutters so I could see the moonlight, I crept into his arms like a lost child and cried myself to sleep.

In those faraway days of early marriage, the halcyon days of my private life in the Fair Bay, Casa da Vinci held me to its charms. I soon discovered the sun to be a bitter enemy. My skin could not bear the burning heat and at night mosquitoes tormented me. It took time and a mosquito-net before my tantrums about being bitten ceased. I learnt to stay out of the sun as much as possible and to have a kind of respect for the fierce command the climate was to have over my life in India.

I spent long hours in the house with my mother-in-law and ayahs preparing a second wedding reception. The first had been given by my parents in London. It was a time of honeymoon and pleasure to be spent with my husband, when we were able to be alone. But the East is full of gregarious, loving souls who thought our honeymoon rather a joke and refused to give in to our plea for privacy. Till we escaped to the hills after the wedding reception was over.

My wing of the house faced the seafront, where a low sea-wall curved along a small pebble beach, that rolled down to the waters edge. Sometimes a small stray pup would splash and swim in the sea, but mostly it was humid and quiet.

Bombay was there waiting to be explored. After the wedding-party, after the endless visits to homes of long-lost relatives. After a whole new family had entered my life. Bombay would open up to me. The Great Mother would show me a larger family. A people once part of an empire I had learnt about at school, would smile on me a slow smile of tolerant greeting. The silver spoon in my mouth had been filled with spiced sugar. But the Great Mother and the gods were watching my every move. Soon to reach out and try to grasp my spirit. To play on my sub-conscious mind and say over and over again, 'Come and join the people, come and see the deprived and unblest creatures of the dark, come and wander through the tangled webs of Indian culture'. But not yet, not yet. Time for awhile to be young and free. To be a bride, to look forward to a reception held under tropical night skies. To wear beautiful clothes and to be unashamedly adored. Too soon the Great Mother would show me her wares of lost humanity and her tune of anguish would become mine.

I suppose everybody who was anybody came to our wedding-night gala held in the grounds of the turf-club. My husband was a compulsive race-goer, so this pleased him very much. To think his wedding reception was held near his beloved horses.

The trees were a mass of fairy-lights. The Goan band played on and on, as I stood with my in-laws and husband, beneath an archway of marigolds and tiny roses. My hair had been brushed by an ayah till every hair was as black as the night sky and my gossamer-white sari woven with silver thread matched the moonlight.

Presents were collected by the basketful as friends, family and other guests arrived. Servants stood next to me to take the gifts from my hands. Money in envelopes and packets of every size was given to my father-in-law.

It is a Parsi custom not to eat with the diners at a function given for others. We walked around the long banquet tables and thanked everyone for coming and I shook hundreds of willing hands, some of them slightly greasy from too much delicious meat eaten with gusto and there fingers.

I remember a happy scene of dancing couples as flowers moved their heads in time to the Goan band's lazy beat. The rich food and Indian perfumes drifted through the night air, as jewels gave off a glitter of gold and gems, worn with perfect ease by women used to richness in clothes and life.

The Parsi women over the centuries they have been in India, wear the sari with great style, their hair is usually short, but the older women wear the bun.

At last the reception had been given. Everyone at Casa da Vinci was pleased. It had been a huge success. Parties were really an every night event if we wished to go to them. Nearly all the celebrities of the day who came to Bombay met the Wadias and from those early memories of mine, I remember Hollywood stars like William Holden to that delightful monkey-faced Sherpa Tensing who had stood on the top of the world, when Everest was conquered. To politicians in and out of government and endless film premieres, meetings with writers and poets and musicians and last, but not least university professors. They came in and out of Casa da Vinci, like the tropical butterflies that flew in and out of the rooms, from the open windows that backed onto the gardens.

My thoughts were not really very active. I was at the first thrill of experience. Busy receiving endless eastern images into myself. It was my own festival of sight. My sight gathered costumes and peoples, scenes filled with atmosphere. Almost a painter's world and I've often wondered since, why painters from the West do not go to India more, just to paint. A city of colours, which leap onto a canvas, pictures of faces and bodies coming from a history deep with intrigue and battles and dancing and glory and pain and death.

And then, the Cries of India. The sounds of Bombay. Of speech and birds and beasts. Of beating drums and weird music from string instruments with ancient names. The sounds of sea and wind and grasshopper's wings.

In the house the sounds of swishing saris and the gentle pit-a-pat of bare feet on marble floors. Of bathroom showers falling over my naked, hot body, and the sounds of my husband's friends laughing at my jokes about India.

Sights and sounds. The early footsteps of my journey. Time to think of the silent world of Indian mysticism. To touch the jogi with my hand and feel his cosmic mind tremble like a fragile leaf.

Every day the leaf unfolded. Every hour a small delicate petal fell from the flowers and still the fans twisted to the heat of the moment and the house stood gleaming in the high noon sunshine.

I swatted flies and drank iced juice, as the ayahs sang old village songs and the kitchen boys ground the spices for their Khana*.

French cooking was enjoyed by the family at home. Indian and Parsi dishes were served only at large dinner-parties. I thought this rather a pity, as I did not think Goan cooks knew very much about European cooking, but they did understand what made up a good curry.

The head house-boy always served our meals in the blue dining-room, where the walls were enpanelled with paintings of old sailing ships as of course the Wadias were ship-builders from ages past.

In his spotless tunic and turban Madu would wait behind our chairs, not flicking an eyelid as we ate and chatted away our meals. Fruit was always served, usually ripe papaya, to aid digestion. After spice, small sweet cachous were offered, to freshen ones breath or small, hard nuts were handed from delicate carved boxes.

Sometimes against the walls a green lizard would sit and watch us eat. I felt he had a sense of humour with his cold eyes just daring to glint. What was a splendid dining-hall to him. This primeval creature whose past mind could share great volcanic eruptions with the dinosaurs and who no doubt remembered the Ark and the floods of the whole world.

The family spoke fluent English although Gujarati was their mother tongue. My father-in-law was very erudite and whenever I could find him at home and not too busy, I'd listen to his stories about Hindustan. We'd sit in his study lined with his books amid leather chairs of pale yellow and a huge desk. This was one of my favourite rooms in Casa da

*Khana — Dinner.

Vinci. I spent hours reading his books and dreaming of the day I would write my own.

He talked of the beauty of Sanskrit poetry, its almost total perfection in verse. He talked of the past glory that was India three thousand years ago, before so much misery fell upon her. He talked of idolatry and Zoroaster, the religious founder of the Parsi faith. Coming from a background of Judao Christianity myself, I would argue with him that Zoroaster was only pseudo-revelation and he would laugh and say that he was an agnostic anyway, but it was nice to talk of such things. We spoke about the Raj, when he was offered a Knighthood, but refused it. He spoke of everything under his Indian sun and I listened and thought of 'cabbages and kings', but didn't think my father-in-law would see the fun in that. My husband's mother was arrogant. She hated me giving money to beggars and although the Parsis first came to Bombay in 1670, I think she felt very Persian and never completely at home. The street urchins certainly did not touch or move her to compassion of any kind. Yet she was a gentle and lovely person. Maybe too much privilege had removed her humility and replaced it by indifference.

I was soon to go on a holiday away from the city. I was by now in the first months of pregnancy with my first child and we went to Matheran, which is only fifty-four miles from the Fair Bay. It is a jungle and hill country, where views of Bombay show up between groups of dark trees. No cars are allowed. Only horses and rickshaws drawn by native hill-men. After a long walk I took one of the rickshaw rides, just before sunset and the poor driver could not find our bungalow and seemed very worried and lost. A search party with blazing torches had set out to look for me. The only words of English the rickshaw-wallah spoke were, 'sit down, Memsahib' and each time I tried to get up to find the correct pathway, he told me to sit down again! I feel this episode was an adventure, as panthers roam the hills at night and green tree snakes hang from branches. But my husband said when he found me again, 'that I never did have any sense of direction'.

Baboons climbed into my bedroom and plastered the

dressing-table mirror with my face-creams and splashed my perfumes everywhere. They are born trouble-makers, full of male-chauvinism, as in the pack the males treat the females to brutish bites and pinch all the best peanuts.

A funny old steam tramway takes everyone up and down to Matheran. Some of the local hill-women wear very little, apart from heavy silver neck and feet ornaments, but you have to be quick to look at them as they climb the slopes in great hurry as if all the male baboons were after them!

In the market place I bought an old copy of D.H. Lawrence short stories, so one never knows where books turn up. But I suppose there are worse places than jungly hills thousands of miles from nowhere!

Back at Casa da Vinci, as my mother-in-law played cards with her friends, I lay almost bedridden with pregnancy sickness. I was miserable, ill-tempered and homesick. My gynaecologist would only allow me to sip cold lemonade as drugs to stop vomiting may have harmed my unborn baby. Yet Vinci nursed me through horrible attacks and my ayah helped me bath. All thoughts about India were for the moment reasonably forgotten, and I threw my shoes at anyone who dared tell me the peasant women had their babies in the rice-fields and went back to work at once!

After the rains my once flat stomach became a bump, as if so much water had made it grow and I could feel my bundle of future joy moving and kicking.

Cyra my daughter was born in London. She was a perfect baby girl with eyes like black-cherries and hair of silk. Cyra is from the latin Cynarae, which means enchantress. She was an autumn baby; the season of Sharada in India. His Highness The Maharaja of Bundi* peeped into her small hospital cot and said, 'All babies look like small kittens,' and they do.

I looked down at my first-born and with tired, dreamy thoughts remembered the battle of the kites I'd seen in the sky just before I left the Great Mother to return to England for Cyra's birth. The kites were all really paper-gods chasing each other across heaven. It was a festival of kites. And then after a long journey of travel, marriage and birth, I was a mother. 'I am your mother,' I said to my sleeping infant. Then I too fell asleep. Very complete, as all the flowers in my

*Sadly His Highness died in 1977 whilst lunching at Broadlands with Mountbatten. He died one day before we were due to meet to discuss the book I had hoped to write on the Indian Princes.

room turned into paper-kites and fled across the sky.

COME GODS LET US GO AND BUY FRUIT

Come you lazy gods enough of your festivals, it is time to do a little shopping. The fruit market, Crawford Market is in the heart of the old city. The very Indian Mumbai. Untouched by any other hands than those of the east. Where narrow streets, become even more narrow, where Muslims wander about wearing clothes that draped the heros from the pages of the Arabian Nights.

Where dark eyes hide behind veils and a mysterious feeling runs through the veins and makes me just a bit afraid of the sinister and unknown streets.

Wooden fronted houses with projecting storeys are covered with carvings and from the old mosque a Mulla* is calling the faithful to come and pray. From the teeming pavements and gaudily decorated houses, they with total obedience to Allah, obey him.

In-between the jumble of property and people, Hindu priests from their Temple, jingle brass bells, also calling their own to worship. It is a day of tolerance, before the sun is twelve o'clock high, amid all the weaving in and out of the back streets, by an endless throng of beings. It is hard to see or feel a fierce hatred of Hindu and Muslim for each other. And Partition of India seems wrong on such a morning as this.

But, no politics. Are you still with me gods or have you become bored with my browsing here and there and turned yourself back into stone?

Half-way into the market a dark-skinned urchin of about seven or eight offered to carry my shopping for me. The basket on top of his head was, I'm sure bigger than both of

*Mulla — Muslim Priest

us, but what could I say? He was too young to work, he was too small and too thin, but his need knew no argument; so off we both went to buy fruit. For him to see me carry my own shopping was unthinkable. I thought I'd buy a little so that he would not have too much to carry on top of his small, black head.

It was easier said than done to buy less fruit. Crawford Market is a still-life painting. A masterpiece that has not been framed and hung. Every stall has fruit and vegetables piled high in a colourful pyramid of polished splendour. Fruit so clean, that one can hardly believe it could be bought in the midst of a rather filthy city. Dozens of brown hands offered to sell me the fruits of Eden. Apples glowing ruby red from the cool orchards of Kashmir. Cherries and grapes. Huge purple melons, greeny-yellow pawpaws, pineapples such as the West has never seen. Strange nameless fruits used for even stranger medical cures. Soft tasting peaches and passion-fruits to keep the libido throbbing. Fresh, ripe figs surely the most sensuous fruit of all. And bunches of red and green cooking bananas and mountains of yellow ones.

There seemed to be no special season for these fruits. They were there by magic or was it by command of the gods? All the fruits of the world, but not the mango. That ever delicious bright orange pulp, really does have a season. May is mango time in Bombay, when the Great Mother becomes almost a furnace of heat, during the hot season, before the rains break. The smell of the mango is so refreshing that it is thought to restore energy to those in a declining state of health and give them added wisdom and enlightenment.

The vegetables looked slightly out of place, but no less beautiful. Freshly picked and washed cauliflower in Crawford Market, has again that same touch of magic about it and I've no doubt that some weird and wonderful magician from one of the quaint wooden houses uses the white-heart to mix love-potions for lovesick Muslim girls.

Lovely birds, cages and all were thrust into my hand. Even a monkey. Selling, selling, selling. With this dear child yelling at me, 'You take, you take, Memsahib, all good, I carry'. A super-salesman at the age of eight getting his cut from the fruit-seller with one blind eye.

Breathless and almost back into the open street, just turning my head once more to look at the flowers and the drinking fountain. And to gaze up at the massive iron roof that covers the whole market. The flowers of India, lilies and marigolds, bright red splashes of tropical petals drooping from long, slender, green stalks, that only a very clever botanist, could possibly know their names.

Tucked away almost forgotten in a corner, were tanks of tropical fish, swimming in their true environment. The water naturally warm, all the colours of rare gems, a moving poem.

By now as I walked back to my car the smells of curry and incense, were coming from every back-street cooking pot. From the open windows I glimpsed families eating their lunch together.

The sun was beginning to torment me and the black flies were sticking to my hot legs. Every beggar in the old quarter knew I was shopping and all were whining at me for alms.

The seats of my car were hot against my back and my eyes were sore, with looking at so much colour. Fruit and flowers and vegetables and fish and birds, were imprinted upon my sunglass' lens. For awhile I had become bound up with an eastern morning of shopping and crowds and I felt drained as the eastern atmosphere, pulled at my strength and left me limp.

I gave all my small change to my little helper and also a bag of Kashmir cherries. He knew I was hot and bothered and his thoughts and mine were separated by a culture so far apart. But his eyes and mine held for a split second the same twinkle.

Even in all this confusion of wealth and poverty and it's believed this triangle of streets holds much of the peninsula's wealth, my little urchin had a sense of humour. With a shrug of his thin, narrow shoulders and a quick, restless nod of his head towards the gods, he dived into the bag of cherries, stuck a couple into his mouth, which was one wide smile.

Then he disappeared into the mass of Gujarati and Mahratta people, that were sprinkled here and there with the Muslims and wandering Jews.

b

THE JANGLE OF GOLDEN BANGLES

Upraised and lovely Indian womanhood. A beauty that calls out of the warm heat that surrounds and shelters it. A promise of the night and a sighing for the moon, all touched by the deep, golden splendour of Indian richness.

The tall, supple girls from the North. A pride to their handsome menfolk and their ancient family traditions. The Rajputs historic and proud; with the blood of warriors and warrior-princes flowing in their veins. With romance and chivalry adding to the glory of their background.

The womanhood of the Sikhs. Pure to their religion, their name means a brotherhood, The Khalsa, purity of faith. These women move like goddesses coming down to earth from white clouds. Their hair flowing streams of black satin, their long legs giving off the merest hint of loveliness hidden beneath their loose, silk trousers.

The small, black beauties of the South, with features going back into ages past and nearly forgotten. Dravidian and wild. And the women from temple-carvings with breasts that have been sculptured by hands that knew and understood, all there was to ever know and understand about female beauty.

The statues of Ajanta and Ellora Caves, from dark antiquity, mingling Buddhist and Hindu beauty into stone. To last as long as forever is.

From hundreds and hundreds of villages, hard working village girls show off their beauty, wearing long, bright handwoven skirts and tight bodices, all dyed with the colours of the rainbow. Their silver ankle bracelets, rings and bangles, heavy earrings and nose-ornaments shine and jingle with the breeze, as they carry water in tough brown pots on their heads or bend low in the rice-fields. Their movements are full of grace, their backs straight and black-cherry eyes fringed with silk lashes look ahead towards their villages, as they walk their children home.

From the humble street-sweeper to the high born women in their exquisite mansions, the same graceful body movement is seen, blended by delicate palm trees, that seem to keep time with the swaying bodies.

Sadly the women of Gujarat do not seem to have been blessed with the legendary female Indian beauty. Mostly the joke is that the 'bain of Gujarat' is the flat chest, and the women seem rather wan. Maybe it is the deep heat of the burning plains that saps the vital spark from their personalities. Perhaps their Hindu caste culture makes each and everyone of them conform to the set rules of life, that has been ordered for them from one generation to another for centuries.

Caste convention gives security to them, within their own caste structure. But makes for the inevitable boredom that comes from never breaking the rules. Even in their homes, which are peaceful and hospitable, there seems little zest for real living. No spontaneous laughter even the educated hold back, giving out no extrovert demonstration in the sense of pure fun from body and mind. Maybe this is very 'Indian', but there is a miss; a vital link needed to quicken life and thoughts to action and living.

In the joint-Hindu family homes, where the generation-gap known in the West does not exist, as whole family units live under one roof from old grandparents to cousins so many times removed, most members have no count of who is really who and it does not matter. A vein flowing with family blood is as holy as precious Ganges water and much thicker. The women seem to be silent, always walking on marble floors, almost nun-like. Quietly helping to prepare vegetables in the kitchens or slowly brushing and oiling their hair.

Still very few of the wives have careers outside the home and the life-style is a continuous pattern of sameness. The identical golden marriage bangles, jangle rhymes to the cowboy Krishna. Their placid eyes give out a kind of anguish. A paradox amid their peaceful 'namaste'*. Pictures hung with reverence against white walls are Holy pictures of Krishna. Their preservation they owe to him and he smiles down on them. A blue-grey young, eighth incarnation of Vishnu. The deity of preservation in the Hindu trinity.

So the women of Gujarat, the coconut oiled, black bunned, un-liberated women of Bombay's suburbs are through their arranged marriages preserved and watched over from the cradle to their last Hindu rites, when the ashes that were womanhood return to the gods. They pass the pattern of existence on to the children and what they did not do in this life, they shall achieve in the next or even the next. Just as all their lives of past incarnations have been answered for Time and Time again, so it shall be unto their final perfection. All their re-births touch their pretty ringed hands and they eat their rice and dhal wih bored satisfaction.

The young wives obey their husbands, supreme lord and master. The veritable saint in his life is his mother. She is also the head of the joint-family line and sadly nearly always a widow. The men do not seem to live very long lives. The wives accept it all knowing in turn they will be adored by their sons, will bring their daughters up to keep all the rules and one day themselves will be mother-in-laws of might and very little mirth.

In a poverty stricken country, where hunger and famine strike the bodies of countless millions, the law of Krishna is wise.

The Preserver knows no better argument for his case against disharmony in the home, than the plight of the poor low caste creatures in the city streets and backward villages. The homeless wanderers, who live like broken promises. Down-trodden humans with no idea of their basic Human Rights, whose ignorance forbids them to cry out. They hide away at night in pipes that are laid for sewage and when the pipes have gone they will find other hiding places.

Untouchable is a word the Great Mother turns her head from. It is enough for middle-class wives to shell peas at home and brush kohl onto their own children's eye-lids to protect them from the evil-eye of disaster. They do not care to discuss the starving babies. The Untouchables and Unseeables are set apart. Fate decided their existence, before they were born and to the Hindu wife anything unclean is also un-talked about.

Mahatma's message of 'love each other' lies buried in the sand. If there is a wind of change blowing across the Sub-Continent it has not blown through the streets or homes of the Fair Bay. But Hinduism knows little action. There is no urgency in what is after all everlasting. No action today in what may have its ultimate meaning a hundred centuries from now. And the pipe dwellers, gentle sufferers bound to their Dharma,* may become perfect saints in an age beyond moon and stars of this small hour. So the pigeons fly above all their black shiny heads and the fishing boats drift along the bay.

A small boy plays an ancient tune on a penny bamboo flute and a house-boy goes to buy a single cigarette from a shack-shop in the side of a wall. He stands and smokes it outside his master's house watching the smoke curl towards the pigeons pale grey wings. He too asks few questions and in turn receives just as few replies.

As the presence of the burning sun is taken for granted so poverty is also taken for granted. Bombay, our Great Mother, has a funny shape, rather like all mothers, who have too many children. Its like a drooping claw that's about to pick up the Konkan coast and take it somewhere else.

Who knows, one day the same claw may pick up all the stricken victims of caste and place them on a lotus leaf planet where there is no more hunger and where Krishna the cow-boy has at last learned in his wondrous world of miracles to save the poor and wash their feet and make endless rice-grains pour down from his distant heavens — just from five grains. After all it was done with loaves and fishes in another time, another place.

As the slim, supple, sari clad women place their morning fruit offerings before Krishna's shrine let their morning prayer be for the poor of the city.

*Dharma — Duty.

THE BOATMAN'S SONG

The slow, Scots steamboat gathered a little more speed. Sailors changed from navy-blue into tropical brilliant white uniforms as flying fish true to their name, flew upon the surface of the waves.

I was sailing back to Bombay with my daughter, who was now almost two-years old. Instead of a splendid P&O liner, with all the Somerset Maugham characters on board, that I had come to know so well, I chose a small one-class ship.

My husband had flown to Bombay almost six months before my sailing date and letters waited for me at ports of call, with urgent requests for me to hurry-up and bring Cyra to see her grandparents for the first time.

The slow boat to Bombay did not even carry a passenger-list. There were no colonials anymore, but interesting groups of geologists going out to the oil-fields of Pakistan. Nursing nuns returning to their missionary hospitals in poor villages in the heart of India, where Hindu or Muslim would denounce their 'good news' with a shrug of dark, lean shoulders, but say, 'it may be so'. They are accepted for the kind women they are, but by many even their medicine is considered 'unclean'.

Other passengers had with obvious delight abandoned their everyday real selves, as the ship's atmosphere of, at times, intense heat, overpowered them into lazy, happy and highly alcoholic people.

Travellers, who turned the world into their own sugar-loaf and sucked it dry like the small, native children sucked their sugar-cane sticks. Knaves all of them, but it was a time of wit and Jolly-Boat laughter. A time of will-o'the-wisp happenings, lost in an instant and valued in a special place of remembering.

A violent sand storm blew from the desert as the ship waited in the oven of hot air that Ismailia had become, before it was our turn to be piloted through the Suez Canal.

Our bodies were scratched and sore with sand and everr-one rushed for their salt-pills. It was a sterile, bleak outlook from the middle of the red-sea with only a glimpse of mountains in the sun-hazed distance. It was too hot to go on an excursion to buy lucky Egyptian scarabs in the Cairo gift-shops, but I stood on the highest deck to find by chance a touch of breeze and watched nomadic families walking along the banks, half hidden by date-palms and swaddled in black, ugly looking blankets. Their few goats bleating after them and their long walking staves digging up the sand.

Maybe this was the very spot, where the Israelites guided by Moses crossed the Red Sea. Who can tell or as the Hindu's say 'it may be so'.

The British drank themselves into almost total discord with the Americans on board and there were profound boozy arguments about of all things, how to pronounce potato, and one should say phonograph and not record-player and we all knew it was Hi-Fi anyway!

The Americans said everything was filthy and the crew drank themselves into the next port. Apart from the Muslims and the nuns the boat was tipsy from one cabin to the next. As we all changed the Time on our travelling-clocks and the old mail-steamer kept up a steady rate of knots heading for Karachi.

Along with all the other children my daughter had prickly heat and refused to sleep at night, because she was too hot. But I smothered her with kisses and anti-itch talc, as once more the East had seduced me away from the West.

Our deck quoits fell into the laps of the smiling nuns who sat quietly watching us at play, thinking quite rightly, that we were all a little touched by the sun.

To keep cool during the nights we'd lie on the freshly scrubbed deck. Talking about ourselves till the dawn light took the stars away. We'd talk about our travels, our countries, our hopes and dreams, the world today and tomorrow. The good, long talks of late nights with relaxed company.

There was no racial tension. Only a togetherness of those

who sail on ships. A very large sea surrounded us. It could overpower our little steamer in seconds. We knew the gods were cleverer than us and the waves gave out a message of flowing waters.

The camels of Suez seemed to remind us of a distant oracle coming from the Pyramids of Gizeh.

A tall Mussulman lay his dark body next to mine and sang the Boatman's Song —

> *We are forgotten like shining foam*
> *What is hope, but a fairy palace*
> *Built on shifting sand,*
> *As the roots of life hang*
> *And float in the wind.*

I would sail on many ships. The articulate flatterers of the hour would bring their offerings. But nothing can dishonour this moment of remembering. The steamboat to Bombay, where our minds were to plunge into the rivers of life as the boatman pledges us to Fate.

A WALK BEFORE SUNSET

Just before it is really dark and the silver moon begins her climb to the top of the sky, families who have been house-bound during the day's heat enjoy an early evening stroll.

Chaupati beach, where politicians shout their half-truths to the masses is now a simple playground. Husbands and wives amble along with children and ayahs. The balloon seller stands waiting for the children to come and buy the bright coloured shapes of nothingness, that float above his head. A fairytale scene of children and donkey rides and coconut drinks fresh from the nut and ice-cream cones of pink or white and little bags of hot pulses, spicy nuts and peanuts for the birds.

Even slightly burned corn-on-the-cob at this evening buffet on the warm Bombay sands. The Great Mother pampers her children. The Arabian Sea is laid out for them like another kingdom as they paddle and toss sea-shells across the waves.

Others wander about the Hanging-Gardens, also part of a fairy-story with a giant shoe from Disney Land for the children to play in. 'The old woman who lived in the shoe, had so many children, she didn't know what to do', suddenly becomes The Great Mother herself, filled to the brim with children who in turn become The Fair Bay, seen in all her beauty from the height of the Hanging Gardens. There she is in early evening; a tropical jewel.

Cries of 'Bas, Bas', from the ayahs, which means 'enough'. To the constant moving of their hands and heads till they look as if they will drop off. 'Jaldi Kao', 'make haste, make haste, it's time for tea' and the little ones chorus back, 'alright, alright, we're coming', in so many different tongues.

Urdu, Sindhi, Marathi, Hindi, Gujarati and more dialects than I could ever believe were spoken.

Happy children with enormous eyes and brushed hair, wearing brief and simple cotton clothes. Some of them wearing light wool cardigans to keep off any sign of chill in the air.

The slightest draught might mean a fever in a city, where illness may lead to foul sickness. So the first sniffle the ayah hears is enough to have spicy, herb tea poured down a child's throat no matter the strong protest. All the while the ayah shouting, 'Now baby, just a little more, thora, thora, just a little more' and down it goes frightening away the most deadly germs. The ayah is now delighted 'Shabash, wonderful, now you will be well. Tomorrow evening is time for another stroll. It's becoming chilly. Time to go home. Darkness is everywhere. The sound of a sitar can be heard, maybe it's Ravi Shankar rehearsing for a concert.

QUEEN OF NIGHT

The noise of the daytime crowds had become a peaceful, tropical calm. A cool breeze blows across the city and the homeless are already sleeping on the warm pavements, curled around ragged blankets.

Only the palms bend and sway their clumsy heads, till the coconuts, almost touch the ground. Even the millions of crows have shut-up cawing and chattering green parrots are tucked away in green branches of sheltering bushes.

Now is the moment for the romantics to stand and stare high into the dark eastern sky, alive with stars and a moon, almost too perfect to describe.

Now the Great Mother becomes the eternal mistress of night. Bombay at night is the mistress of the heart. The everlasting young Venus, touched by desire and loved by a universe of starry lovers from heavens unknown realms of gold and silver light.

Colours unbelieved to human sight float from the sky. Burning gold-fires, reds and gently greens, almost cannot be told. Shadowed only by the secretive blackness of the warm night itself. All a poet's wonder of delight. A poet's dream. Swimming through a sea of mist that darkness brings with a kiss from heaven. Mistress of night. Bombay of lover's fantasy, many stand and worship from the earthy temple of night-time streets. Many moon-struck, hypnotised, worshippers stand and are held, forever captive to the moon and stars.

The pleasure-seekers are tempted. Along Marine Drive traffic moves towards the night life. Air-conditioned clubs and restaurants, each one more enticing than the one before, offer food and peep-shows, music and surprises!

Asians and Europeans, Americans, the world, hold hands over delights of eastern sensuality. All hoping The Karmasutra will unfold for them its dark pages and they may discover the mystery that lies beneath layers of Indian erotica.

Suddenly, the night is even darker and the air, becomes heavy with exotic perfume. Queen of Night the lovely, little white blossom of a flower is opening up and filling the city with perfume. Pure white jasmine, fragile and tender. Children sit for hours tying these flowers of night through strands of string. Hindu women then buy the decoration to tie into their buns. The fragrance is a blending of lily-of-the-valley and rare perfumes from Egypt all blended together with rose petals, to become Queen of Night.

I covered my wrists with Queen of Night and wished I had a black bun twined with silver thread and heavy with the perfume of these flowers. I felt the magic of eastern cities after dark stir my blood and tinge my imagination with the promise of love.

Yet another queen reigns in Bombay's night. She too offers the eternal mistress praise. She twinkles and blinks the night away and circles the huge bend of Marine Drive, which forms part of the bay, where the Arabian sea laps the sands of Chaupati beach.

The Queen's Necklace. Hundreds of lights that shine around the bay and look like a priceless pearl necklace on a dark-skinned queens throat. Even Sheba would have worn this trinket with pride.

Two queens in this eastern city. Lights and perfume bending emotions towards the everlasting mistress of the moon and stars and harbour sounds.

The Queen's Necklace glitters with enchantment and the flowers bind a heart. The limbs feel weak, as the night people gather together to dance beneath a heaven of diamond stars. Come gods and goddesses from your temples and join the queens of Bombay. Let us dance together.

TEMPLES, CAVES, LAKES
and
THE COMING OF THE KING

My husband's family were not Parsis of orthodox faith. No pictures of Zoroaster hung from the walls of Casa da Vinci. No food taboos were observed and the household was run by old and trusted Christian or Hindu servants.

No one went off into corners to meditate. There was no ringing of bells, chanting of hymns in bedroom-shrines and no one covered themselves with sesamum oil.

And when my father a well-worn traveller came to Bombay on a business trip to buy precious stones and to meet the Wadias, he met a highly educated, cosmopolitan family born to an elite way of life, who talked with nostalgia for the old Parsi grandeur. The younger generation of men seemed to enjoy Europe more than staying home to add to their wealth and acquisitions.

It's difficult to buy gems in India, because the sunlight often makes glass look like the real thing. But my father said, 'no cunning oriental' would trick him into buying glass. And so we all waited for the jeweller to come to the house with his treasures. I had become so used to Indians crying their wares and appearing with baskets on top of their heads filled with fish or fruit, that I half expected a merchant to arrive with a basket load of priceless gems neatly placed on top of his coconut-oiled head. But, no, the jeweller came looking rather stern, very Hindu indeed, wearing a long, white coat with a high collar and flimsy dhoti. He sat crossed-legged on the floor in front of my father and spread a small collection of star-saphires, rubies and emeralds upon a white sheet. The gems were priced and weighed and spied at through jeweller's eye-glasses, as the talk went into lakhs of rupees.

The fabulous gems would soon be in London, but in this solemn moment as the merchant sipped iced lime and folded his white linen sheet up, my husband quipped, that he'd bet a hundred chips, at least one piece of glass had exchanged hands! My father refused to laugh, as the jeweller placed his brown hands together and gave us the traditional sign of farewell and thank-you!

I became an unpaid guide and took my father on a tourist outing, showing off the Fair Bay and the usual places of interest to foreigners. He had arrived by ship and thought the first views of Bombay harbour as good as Naples. I told my driver to take a weeks holiday and gave the keys of the car to my father and as drops of perspiration fell from his bald sunburnt head, together we became explorers.

We both thought The Mahalakshmi Temples could have been cleaner. One, almost naked priest looking like an over-fed orang-outang, lay cluttered up around the intricate carvings in a state of semi-divine repose. I was sure a temple prostitute had just paid him homage and left him lying near a warm pool of ghi*, fatigued yet refreshed!

The supernatural commands its own respect no matter one's private thoughts. Man, myth and magic, idols and gods coming from the dark ages of a worlds beginning.

Beggars stroked our backs with their bandaged limbs, as the temple gods and goddesses lay horizontal in each others arms. A thin cow with decorated horns left a prized puddle of urine near our feet. The air was heavy with sandal-wood, Hindus offered up their devotions to Lakshmi, their foreheads striped with sect marks and a serene vision of cosmic triumph played upon their eyes.

A small craft took us out to the Caves of Elephants, an island about six miles from The Fort of Bombay. My father was slightly shocked at the 4ft lingam shrine. I said, as the father of seven children he should have been more of a sup-plicant and less of a critic.

We drove out to Lonavla to see the lakes. And to the Great Cave of Karli, where the ascent to the cave is 400ft. Bombay's electricity power comes from these lakes and during the rains the waterfall is a glorious sight.

*Ghi — clarified butter

Back in Bombay we went to Wadia—Movie-Tone studios to watch the 'rushes' of a new film. Everyone ate tiffin of cold, spiced omelettes and drank tea. The film-stars looked uncomfortably hot in heavy silk costumes and thick make-up. Acting yet another epic for the Indian screen, of Indian history, blood-thirsty, very cruel and full of celluloid heroes.

It was almost the time of goodbye. I took my father to buy curios and khaddi cloth and to see the statue of Sivaji, the great hero founder of Mahratta power, who sits waving his sword on the back of a huge horse. He is such an adored hero, I could not let my father leave India, without taking a photograph of him and the statue, near the Gateway of India, and surrounded by a deep blue sea.

Then only leaving a ribbon of vapour in the hot sky the jet was gone and my father smiling and wearing with charm the garlands we had all covered him with, had left the Fair Bay to return home to London for Christmas.

It was now almost Shishira the cold season. I taught the cook how to roast a chicken for Christmas dinner and I bought a bright green plastic Christmas tree, which delighted my daughter and Rosie the old Christian ayah, who had nursed my husband as a boy and now spoiled our daughter.

There had never been a Christmas celebration at Casa da Vinci and my husband was an atheist to his last pair of gold cuff-links, but all the East admires a good festival.

Crackers were pulled, presents exchanged and Christmas cards from England and Indian friends covered the walls.

At midnight Mass an unknown Jesuit father was the celebrant and in the morning we greeted the Coming of The King with a sign of peace, as family and servants alike kissed each other Happy Christmas.

ALONG A STRETCH OF SAND

A few dusty miles outside Bombay is one of the loveliest untouched beaches in the world. Juhu. Miles and miles of good firm sand and great thinly bending palms by the Arabian sea, hot and dark blue.

Where its an early morning beauty to see the red and white sailed fishing dhows coming in with the catch.

Strange named Indian fish. Pomflet and palla fish and many others gleaming in the sun. All day Juhu is silent; from dawn the fishermen sort their catch and all along the edge of the sand are tiny gasping fish rejected and dying and rather sad.

A lonely coconut-wallah sits crossed legged his grimy dhoti clinging round his legs, his coconuts full of delicious milk waiting to be drunk.

At noon the sun is fierce and only the brave and perhaps a few English will be seen. But the peace is somehow un-equalled. It is so quiet and calm, not even birds move or sing only shy, fawn crabs run hastily across the sand from one hole into another.

Drying and growing in the sand is cress, which the peasants water and cover with enormous banana leaves till it is ready to gather. Then it is fried and eaten with onions and spice.

A servant takes a dog for a walk. A huddled figure sleeps, all is hot and sticky, even the sea moves without sound.

Then the sun slips into the sea just before the sky is alight with stars. Juhu becomes alive with people.

First the ayahs bringing the children out for the evening walk. Some European with blonde hair, fair against the dark skinned nannies. Some Indian, all running to look at a tame bear parading with its trainer for their fun and their pocket-money.

Shy young Indian couples in love. The girls in cotton saris showing off their caste sign on the forehead and looking very pretty. The boys in white starched trousers and white shirts just daring to hold their girl's hands. Utterly simple not at all the Western approach to love.

Groups of old religious Hindu widows also sit crossed legged on the sand. Their faces genial and full of grace. They chant sutras* while the sun sets. The sun had given the flame and fire to life. They are old now and at peace with themselves, only waiting for the last fire to draw their ashes towards the feet of the gods they praise.

Hinduism has a final victory over their deaths as it held over their lives.

The English walk the dogs, men and women wearing shorts and looking slightly out of place with this Indian throng. Juhu belongs to India. The bungalows of the rich are neatly built along the sides of this huge beach. A grand chi-chi hotel shines white in the sunshine for pleasure loving tourists. But, nearer the sea the bamboo huts of the people sway in the breeze and Juhu gives itself to the walking throng every evening before dusk.

I often wonder what happens on that long, long stretch of sand, when only the stars are there. Perhaps all kinds of weird things. But I don't think so. Juhu is fun and beautiful and made for thousands of bare feet to be covered with sand.

*Sutras — Holy Songs, chants.

THE BLUE CROSS OF FAITH

Very near to Juhu, three miles away, is a small suburb named Bandra. Bandra is a strange sort of place even for India. East meeting West in a jumble-sale kind of way. Neat bungalows and flat roofed dwellings not far from odd shacks with black pigs running wild by the roadside, and naked babies crawling in the dust.

Bandra is the home of Indian Christians, mostly of Anglo-Indian blood. Touched by the Christian faith and set apart. They work as civil-servants, low grade typists, all kinds of office-staff and nurses and sometimes teachers. They commute the seven miles into the centre of the Great Mother by train to Central Station. Hindus and Muslims, rarely do their kind of work.

The other Christians are Portuguese Goanese Catholics, who are house-servants, and cooks. The young girls sew beautifully and are famed for their needlework. They all have a zest for life and young Goans are supurb dancers and good musicians. Bombay nightlife would be dull without their bands and strippers, their fun and laughter.

The Christian in India is absorbed into the flow of Hindu life. Not much fuss or importance is given to them. A blessing in fact from 'Our Lord', because unlike the Muslim and Hindu wars, the Christian has been allowed to worship in quiet neglect. As they are nearly always very poor nobody bothers them. To the Hindu mind they are unclean, but not evil. The first converts were in South India, where it is possible that St. Thomas, the same doubting Apostle, was sent there. He went with great reluctance and founded the Syrian church of South India.

St. Thomas it is recorded, had a dread of India and wished
The Lord to send him anywhere on earth, but not India. The
Lord has strange ways of working His Will and to India
St. Thomas was sent. It can never be proved, if it was the
blessed Apostle, but I'd love to believe it was. His tomb
'San Thom' in Madras is of course a distance from the quiet
little suburb of Bandra.

The Christians nearly all wear western dress and it looks
like a perpetual Sunday afternoon in an English park in the
early fifties. With girls wearing floral cotton dresses with full
skirts and the men with sleeked down hair. Not many of the
women have Hindu style buns, but they copy the latest hair
fashion from the movies.

The blue-cross of faith is tattooed on their arms or hands
and holy medals are worn around their necks. They are
simple, family minded folk, shaking hands with each other in
the street on Sundays and celebrating feast-days with gentle
love and respect.

The Jesuit Fathers watch over their needs if they are
Catholic and their schools and missions and hospitals are
always packed. Missions from all over the world tend their
flocks as missions always do. The Hindu gods watch it all
and take the offerings into themselves!

Anglo Indians all sound like Welshmen. They speak a
sing-song English. When the British left India, they were left
behind with their traces of English blood, to linger on in
silent despair. Showing off a fridge in their front rooms as a
possession worth display and trying to pretend they are not
Indian in the least.

The Goans have their own culture, but Bandra Christians
live in the twilight of the Cross in a lost world. They pray at
Mount Mary Chapel and come to life at Christmas time, when
the birth of their Saviour is celebrated with joy.

Beautiful frocks and new suits are worn. The children
indeed the whole family, is overdressed. The men hot and
uncomfortable in their dark suits and everyone rather sweaty,
but the hand-shaking goes on for hours. They are proud of
their faith. They all secretly dream of 'going home' to England one day. Many have already left India. It's a shame that
for most of them their 'homecoming' was one of disillusion

and an irony that Christian Bandra of the blue-cross is more charitable and loving than Leeds or Birmingham.

The Mission Fathers try and tell the people to stay by the Arabian sea, where the Great Mother holds everyone in her arms. But humans are restless and seeking and the sun has little mercy. So they leave and find a cold climate is a bad awakening to a dream of home.

THE MESSENGER

Surita's daughter is to be married. As she makes her early morning Puja to the idols in the shrine at the far end of her bedroom, her thoughts, as she places her offerings of marigolds, are of the coming wedding.

Sadness lingers about her, because her husband is dead and will not see their beautiful daughter become a bride. She sprinkles holy water over her adored gods and with peaceful veneration hangs fresh garlands about their necks. She prays for Sushila, her daughter, who will soon leave the household for her new husband's home.

Her own wedding had been noisy and incoherent, as nearly all eastern weddings are. At the end of that long, hot day, how tired, how weary she and Chandu were. And how desperately shy.

Sushila does not seem nearly so shy, but youth is different now or so it seems. Now her daughter would wear the wedding sari. How stiff she had felt in hers. She felt far more comfortable in her morning white cotton sari than she ever did on her wedding day. But she and Chandu were bound to each other for ever and ever.

He tied a ribbon in a knot about her neck. She tied her sari to him. She smiled as she remembered, how she hoped her father would refuse his consent, before Chandu tied the knot, because then the marriage would have been stopped and she could have returned home to her mother. But it was not to be. She and Chandu walked around the Hindu fire, their marriage had been arranged, as all the best marriages are.

From childhood their parents had plotted and schemed to

see them man and wife. Before they could walk or talk the gods decided their destiny. She had grown to love Chandu and he loved her. The sacred thread were wound around their souls.

She stood like a proud Parvati on the right side of Chandu; for as a Hindu wife she could only eat with him and stand at his right side on their wedding day. Parvati, sweet goddess, who at times lost her temper, stood on the right of Siva, when they married. Surita smiled again as pictures of her wedding day crossed her mind. She knew Brahma, priest of the gods, had been there, bringing with him an attendant, bearing a water-pot for the ceremony and Chandu, the moon-god, was waiting to shimmer all the silver of the moon over their first night of love and togetherness.

And how they threw rice over each others head as an offering to the gods, for a future blessing of sons.

Sushila had refused to have an arranged marriage. She wanted to fall in love as they fell in love in the West. The whole family was hurt and bewildered and more than a little angry. The young were stubborn, but they would learn.

All Surita's pleading and tears with her daughter came to nothing. It was fall in love or spinsterhood. Where did she and Chandu find this strong-willed girl, with huge eyes and long black hair. It was Paravati's temper again!

So the mother begged the gods to give her daughter enlightenment and she prayed that her new son-in-law would not disappoint her or the relatives, who had such critical opinions about youth growing up without order and obedience to Caste.

Customs do not give way to emotions; marriages must be arranged. The stars had to be obeyed. Sushila had to learn that social security was security within her Caste. Marry for love she might, but marry outside of her Caste and she may as well die, before nightfall.

So the struggle went on and soon it would be another wedding day. She took a deep breath about it all. Chandu was dead and she had not thrown herself into the flames as widows of old and past times did, but had returned home to her children.

Just before her marriage her father had called the astrologers to their house and she and Chandu had their horoscopes read and re-read so the marriage would take place on the right day. It had to be a happening that was harmonious and pleasing to the gods.

The astrologers agreed the wedding could take place. The pundits had spoken. The union was blessed with children, but a certain darkness would overtake them. This was to be the early death of Chandu, but nobody questioned it. It was a wise union. A daughter had been found a good husband and to her father this was an occasion of great importance. The verdict was accepted and Surita waited for her wedding day. Her mother had fussed about her and talked about marriage. Many aunts and cousins came to the house with knowing smiles and odd bits of gossip about this one's wedding, and that one's first child and this husband's bad points and so it went on for weeks. Jewels were brought from the strong box for her to wear and the household talked nothing, but weddings, till it was almost time for the rains.

From a small girl she had been taught her husband was to be her lord and master. She must not think for a brief second, that she, a mere girl was his equal. The life-pattern in the home meant that she, bound by her marriage vows, would honour his mother, his family, his gods, and his children.

She would take all this into herself and become Srimati or holy-mother, but maybe with her tongue tucked inside her delicate brown cheek. She would tell the world her husband was her lord and master, for in reality this subservience is a fine veil, that once seen through causes mirth and laughter.

The Indian husband is of negative quality and the wife often rules with determination, that young wives in the West are fighting to discover, in the quest for liberation.

Surita's thoughts still sprang memories to life. Chandu and she had in their marriage a mystical happiness. Their souls had met and she gave him all her purity and devotion. He gave her his love and family pride.

In the forests of his first beginning the seed of this union was sown. And even in death his soul remained in the heart of his wife. She was not alone.

She did not care what bargaining had gone on between

their families, when the marriage was arranged, for she wanted to marry Chandu, even though she was shy and afraid and very young. She had not troubled her mind with family plots. She sat at her mothers feet and felt the marble floor cool beneath her. She listened to her mother telling her the old and well loved stories from their ancient heritage. She could hear the echo of her mother's voice rising and falling, as she re-told the golden tale of 'The Messenger'.

In the golden city of Ravana shone a golden palace. Sita wept by day and by night. Her husband, her lord, her beloved Ramchandra was separated from her by war. She cursed her fate with cries and weeping. Utterly desolate in her golden palace, edged with palms, beneath the hottest sun in the world, in her golden city.

All this gold held no fulfilment to Sita the lonely queen, surrounded by pomp and pageantry. Without her Ramchandra, her life was an island cast with monsoon storms. As the heat burned the sides of the golden palace and her servants slept on their woven mats, a messenger sweaty and in great haste threw himself before Sita.

Her eyes dark and lovely, her lashes wet with tears, held a look of relief as the messenger said her husband was safe and had not forgotten his dearest wife. Soon he would rescue her. 'See, this is his ring' the messenger said. At the sight of Ramchandra's ring her mind was reassured. The messenger was telling the truth. Her husband lived. His ring like a love-letter lay in her hand and she could feel her husband's pulse throbbing like her own.

Their wedding ring, the binding of their bodies and ideals, through separation and grief. Their piece of golden heart priceless beyond all golden palaces.

She no longer a queen, only a woman waiting and grieving. Giving all to blind faith for the husband she loved.

A golden city long ago, built on hot sand and stones, below the amazing Indian sun. A black turbaned messenger, bringing the eternal message of the human heart. A golden wedding ring. The message of love through marriage.

Surita let the story blend into her morning prayers. She could feel her mother's fingers gently combing her hair as she told her the story. Now she would re-tell it to her daughter and it would still be fresh and young, because it was eternal.

They would prepare for the wedding together. Deep crimson and gold wedding invitations had been sent to everyone. As she was a widow the card read simply, 'Surita Chandulal invites you to a reception on the occasion of the wedding of her daughter, Sushila to Agit'. To be held at the Gymkhana, Marine Drive, Bombay. She was pleased with the cards and she knew the couple would receive fine gifts and have an auspicious day for their marriage.

As the incense in her bedroom drifted over the shrine and went in narrow puffs of smoke, like violet shreds of silk, to the ceiling, so her prayers went up to her Hindu heaven for her daughter and the young man, soon to be her husband.

The wedding sari was heavy Benares silk and Sushila would look like the goddess Parvati come to life. The wedding car would be decorated with a living mass of white lilies and orange marigolds. It would move through the streets of the Fair Bay like a moving painting. As she dusted the family photographs and placed garlands around those of the dead, she suddenly knew she had always been a romantic at heart.

She had never to make any real decisions of her own. The Caste order of her family, traced the pattern of her destiny for her to follow and obey. And in time Nirvana would be hers.

Even though her marriage had been arranged, at her deep heart's core, one single rose petal could unravel her emotions in a frightening way. She knew her daughter was the same. Falling in love was a tangled path to tread and the thorns from the rose made young flesh bleed.

She doubted if Sushila and Agit would know the peace their parents knew in marriage. Her daughter had exchanged harmony for ecstasy, but it had been the fate of Hindu brides to survive and grow deeply attached to their husbands. But, ah! to be a romantic on a hot night when the moon looks like a shining jewel in the sky.

Gazing at her dead husband's picture and putting some loose strands of greying hair back into her bun and placing a puja mark on her forehead, she thought, 'in this life we had harmony, in the next we shall have romance'. In a drawer, where she still kept one of his kurta tops and dhoti, lay a faded poem called The Hindu Bride, she would give it to her daughter.

> *I have tied my sari to you forever*
> *Six gold bangles ring my arms,*
> *My ears are pierced with bridal earrings*
> *Chapples keep my feet from hot stones.*
> *My oiled bun reflects your face*
> *Around my dark neck gold chains*
> *Say, 'you are my lord',*
> *Krishna will deliver our son,*
> *His name will be Dharmasukh*
> *Or religious happiness.*

And thus the sari is tied to the husband forever. The dance of life is danced around the marriage fire. The Lila, sacred dance of existence before the gods. Krishna will take this offering from the happy couple. The sacred fire will not go out in this life or a thousand lives to come.

Indian women marry and their husbands come to the marriage bed with promises of life written into the palms of their hands and as they take their brides to the hills, for the traditional honeymoon, old Hindu women gossip over spiced tea and chuckle about it all.

NO ROSE WITHOUT A THORN

The impetus of my life was my work. When I first met my husband, I was a last year student at the Guildhall School of Music and Drama. I dared call myself a poet even then and knew my life was bound to typewriter, inkwell and MSS.

I had begun to ask myself questions about my life in Bombay as the first short stabs of restlessness made me think about my real identity. It was not a moment of frenzied homemade psychology, but was I acting out a female-faustian nightmare and losing my soul to high living in the Fair Bay. Would my marriage survive? We were so young. Had the Great Mother with her special benevolence stolen me away from myself?

The gravity of my thoughts made sleep impossible and I stood on my balcony in the middle of the night and watched the mali* watering the lawns, before the sun left the grass faded and parched.

In the moonlight I could see the nightwatchmen who guarded the house talking together and I felt in the morning my conflict would not seem so bad. As the sea gave off a low whining sound I went back to my bedroom and with mosquito-net around me, fell asleep.

And as the morning came, the servants called to each other in loud voices, 'Aj Kya Samachar Hai?' 'What news today?'. A monkey troupe was brought to the garden to entertain my daughter and she clapped and gave them money and nuts, at the end of a very theatrical performance of a mock marriage.

The silence of early afternoon, when the sun blazed high in the cloudless sky, was broken only by a few cawing crows

*Mali — Gardener

and their ugly singing did not assuage my mood.

My husband diagnosed 'homesickness' and suggested the English Club. The English at the club were mostly old Raj veterans with yellow, wrinkled skin from their 30-odd years in the East. They had remained in India after Independence and 'home' to them had always been a six-month leave every three years on a homeward bound P&O boat. The club was an anachronism and I chose to meet my close English friends elsewhere.

I had real fears about Cyra being kidnapped and having her legs crushed and being turned into a beggar. My imagination ran away with itself and my domestic problems became almost insurmountable.

Indian wives use their servants as whipping boys, shouting abuse at houseboys and ayahs. They rarely row with their husbands. All their pent-up household and marriage frustrations are eased off none to gently onto their servants backs.

But I fought, in good old western style, with my husband and we shouted and screamed till it made our marriage look very similar to the mock monkey wedding.

I began to contribute to a monthly literary magazine for All India Radio. Reading my poems, taking voice parts in radio plays and having chat-shows about new books and writers.

Then I became an announcer for English speaking programmes and even had an afternoon record hour.

I could not pronounce Indian place names and with care my husband would go over the script with me and write all the words in phonetics and I'd learn them just before I went over the air.

This work came to my rescue for awhile. It was ludicrous to think I could live in Bombay and just sit on a cushion sewing a fine seam and anyway I loathed sewing.

Nationalism in the studios, when a colleague refused to show me how some equipment worked, because I was British, hurt me a little, but I understood. The British were a delicate subject to talk about and tempers would burst very quickly like a pink Bombay balloon.

My own domestic conflict did not go away. I hadn't the

Snake Charmer

Roadside Hairdressers

"Victoria"

Festivity for some Hindu festival.

Wayside animal show.

Holy (Prescient) bull.

Yet another temple and the cow.

Banana Vendor

A larger clay Ganesh being immersed on Ganesh Chaturthi.

Town Hall (19th Century) now Asistic Library.

Breach Candy Swimming Pool

A portion of Victoria (Railway) Terminus.
Typical turn of the century mock Gothic architecture.

Dhobi Ghat (local laundry) at Mahaluxmi.

Race course from Members' Stand.

Clock Tower ("Rajabai Tower") in the University complex.

Feeding the Holy Cow.

Fisherwomen at a Versova Village well.

Fishing and cargo boats at Mahim.

Roadside circus

Now defunct tram car at Pydhoni Junction.

Fortune Telling for Rs.2 beside Gateway of India.

Evening scene from a quayside.

Coconut Vendor

A circus travelling through Flora Fountain to its new site.

Juhu Beach, Bombay.

(c) Govt. of India Tourist Office

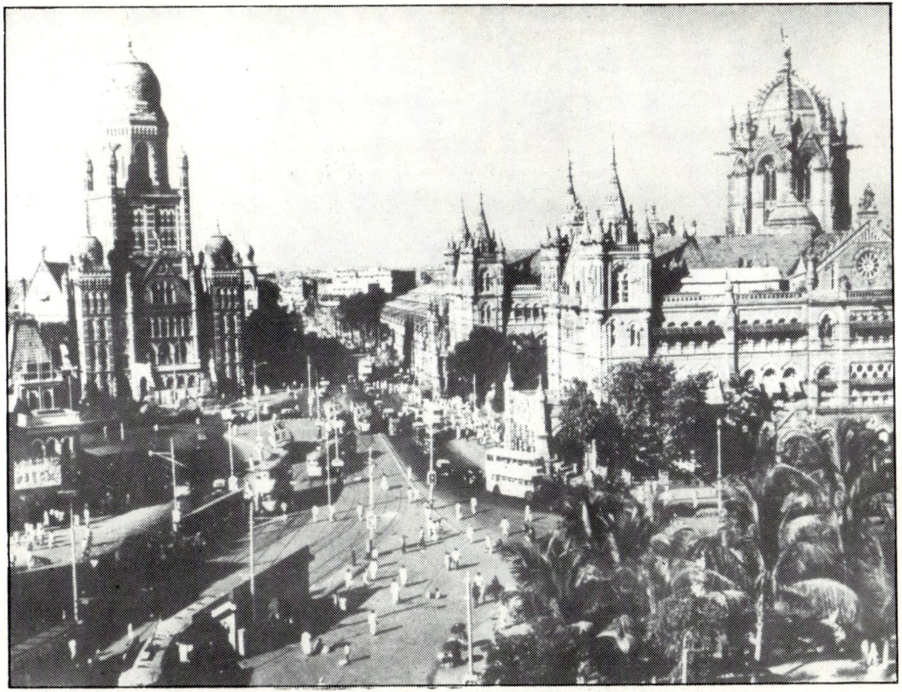

Bombay Railway Station

experience as yet, needed to mould a career and marriage into success. If indeed a writer can achieve this bliss. I think being an author has always been less of a struggle for a man than for a woman.

I did not see enough of my daughter as broadcasting hours were long and erratic. The house was still as lovely. The marble floors glittered against the simple, elegant furniture. Intellectuals came to discuss Cultural Freedom with my father-in-law and as I stepped into my car, Salim, my Muslim driver, would place a freshly picked bunch of roses at my feet.

Yet not very far from the long avenue of large, opulent homes the outcaste families lived in hovels covered with sacking and hungry babies crawled in their own excrement.

Election slogans beat out a message of 'do away with poverty' and the simplicity of rural village life gave way to the diseased and despairing poor. Bombay's uncared for thousands. I thought of the lines of a poem about Versailles in the time of the French troubles.

> *The garden bright with a fairy light*
> *At many a summer fête,*
> *And ruin and famine and death and Hell*
> *Not half a mile from the gate.*

There is no rose without a thorn and Bombay had many thorns, which pricked my skin. My husband said I was too sensitive and that what I called poverty was just a peasants way of life. Then one night as I was leaving the studios of All India Radio I stepped on the dead body of a child, left in the gutter, just near my car. The sorrow of it all spun around my mind like a spinning-top.

The red soil and boiling sun had crusted my life with pity and melancholy. The futile hopes for a better India for the poor and after dinner talks from influential social workers had left me weary. I needed the fields and skies of England. I needed to hear violins sing and woodwinds call.

For awhile the Great Mother had left me a sapless creature. My marriage was over and once again I stood on Ballard Pier and my beautiful child sat on one of our cabin trunks as

c

I checked my passport.

My friends had filled the cabin with flowers and tears burned behind my ears as a noisy band played the liner out to sea. Bombay disappeared leaving a backcloth of sun-scorched mountains against a tropical blue sky.

NO REVOLUTION THAT DAY

Paratroops, bombs and Sir Anthony Eden's gunboats had closed the Suez Canal to British ships. A long, lazy voyage round The Cape of Africa brought me home again. The magnificent Continent was in a cauldron of slow-boil black unrest, and political upheaval.

It happened in Zanzibar the Isle of Cloves. A *coup d'etat* threw out the Sultan and the army took over the island. I remember a day underneath African skies, when Zanzibar was sleepy, dusty, rather pretty and very, very hot.

Everywhere the fragrant smell of cloves and cinnamon crept up my nostrils. The whole island smelled like an exotic pudding waiting for custard to be poured over it.

I toured Zanzibar with a huge, amiable African guide, whose jolly face gave no hint of revolution or that trouble was imminent. His name was George Washington and he said people wrote to him from all over the world, just to 'George Washington, Zanzibar.'

We drove out to the clove plantations and I picked handfuls of fresh cloves and cut tiny pieces of yellowish-brown bark off the cinnamon trees. I dug my fingernails into the tender twigs to release the smell of cinnamon.

Tall young boys were cracking coconuts and selling milk to thirsty tourists and when the guide said their prices were too high, and argument began in native lingo and deadly sharp knives were waved above our heads, I made a quick retreat from the coconut vendor and settled for an arm of bananas instead, which stretched half-way across a narrow street.

The guide carried one end and my daughter the other as mischievous African children plucked the small, delicious fruit, from the arm and ran away laughing.

Outside a mud-hut six tribal women danced a traditional dance of greeting. They were all wives of a Muslim chief, who refused to let me take any photographs of his dancing wives as he believed the camera had evil spirits in it. He almost had me believing it as well. The women moved trance-like in circles. Their black leathery stomachs swaying with the palm trees. From the plantations the drive to the centre of town was all jungle. We jogged up and down on dirty mud-track roads and arrived with a bang in the stuffy square. In the small group of shops Indian merchants were selling all the usual curios. The women that were about all wore purdah and peeping out from their ugly, black drapes I could see ten toes covered with dust.

A few restaurants, a colony of British, a whitewashed hospital, a nun, maybe a cinema. Altogether a quiet place.

Suddenly a great excitement. The gates of a gleaming palace were thrown open and two heralds blew important sounds from golden trumpets. The Sultan of Zanzibar appeared with his Sultana, walking humbly behind him. They climbed into a flame-red Humber car and were driven slowly away into the clove-smelling distance. Some weeks before Princess Margaret had been their guest.

Still clutching my arm of bananas. My hands perfumed with cloves and cinnamon, my eyes aching from too much sun, I drove to the launch that was waiting to take us all back to the liner and Cape Town.

The island grew smaller circled by a deep-blue sea and a sky just beginning to grow dark. The Isle of Cloves was silent except for a few noisy green parrots. There was certainly no revolution that day!

Only George Washington grinning as he showed off his island home. What terrible secrets were tucked up his sleeve as he was being so nice to us British?

It's a shame to think the grand old Sultan is no more. Now the army is plodding all over his palace. Revolutions change everything, well that's what they are for.

But, I think of Zanzibar as an amusing fairy-tale kind of place, where scents came out of twigs and children stole my bananas, when they thought I wasn't looking.

THE CALL OF INDUS

Richmond in mid-summer was warm and the river-views from my waterside flat were of couples walking along the towpaths as rowing boats bobbed up and down. Pairs of white swans floated on the Thames, while from its banks old men sat fishing.

My arms were heavy with pain from tropical jabs. Luggage was everywhere, cables and letters and lightweight clothing littered the chairs.

The Fair Bay from 7,000 miles away, held me like a magnet holds a pin. The Richmond scene passed before the open french-doors. I could already see reflected on the window panes images of water-carriers and pale, thin cows and cobblers squatting outside their shacks.

Indus was calling me back, yet again. I would become a willing spectator amongst her holy bathing ghats and vain peacocks.

I was now the wife of a Bombay High Court lawyer and Daniel, our son, was still a toddler. I was free to travel with my children before their education made demands on my time. The world seemed to be turning around towards a more cosmopolitan unity and I wanted my daughter and my son to be very international in mind and travel.

We sailed, when the monsoon winds still raged in the Indian Ocean and giant waves covered the lower decks. The liner was said to be jinxed, because five passengers had died on board. The superstitious gazed anxiously up at the stars looking for signs of doom. And others prayed for a safe arrival.

An Italian doctor threw himself overboard into the horrific

monsoon waves. The boat was only three days from Bombay. Over the loudspeakers a voice announced, 'man overboard we are turning back to look for him'. Waves give nothing back. The Italian didn't join the ship again and the monsoon sea violent in the tropic night gave out a sad, grim melody of suicide.

Indian streets were once more underneath my feet. For the first time in the tropics I had to learn to run my own apartment. There were no servants that had been with us for years. It was a new marriage, a new way of life in a new part of the city for me. The towering block of flats overlooked a palm-tree bay surrounded by the Arabian Sea. In Napean Sea Road. An upper-class district not far from the Governors residence.

With much laughter and many battles with flying cockroaches the apartment took on the looks of a spacious eastern home. Piece by piece the carpenters brought our furniture all made by hand and one by one, the servants joined us.

Domestics in India for outsiders can be a problem. Caste is a barrier, which does not bend the knee to reason. No bridge of understanding can be crossed to reach difficult situations. Heated arguments if not handled with extreme care, cause trouble and tears.

The servants are born in backward villages and rarely have a mentality higher than, not very advanced twelve-year olds. Some of the Goans can read and write due to Catholic schooling, but nearly all servants are illiterate. They are servants in the cities to retain their village dependents and have no other choice of employment. It's no use pretending servants like waiting on the rich or the idle or foreigners. Underneath the obsequious manner lies a discontented spirit. They return home once a year to see their wives and children and their lives are dull and hopeless.

My husband used to say about our unconventional marriage with its long partings that he felt like a villager seeing his wife once a year.

For a Bombay household our mixture of servants was unique. The children had a Tamil speaking ayah from the South. The bearer was a Marathi speaking, strong, young man. Mary, the ayah, fought with him nearly every day, because like most women she wanted the kitchen to herself. The bathboy refused to clean any floors, because he owned land in his native village. So a sweeper had to be hired to come in every morning to wash the marble floors.

Parsis are never servants, but my chauffeur was a poor Parsi who had fallen on hard times. He was also a devoted friend, and always said I'd get murdered if left alone with what he called 'my bunch of savages' as the apartment was a hubbub of Caste-warfare. But he was a man of little faith and my extraordinary household even with a militant ayah was a fun-place to live in.

Indians have a reverence for books and the written word. Although the nation is about 75% illiterate, as soon as they heard my typewriter, Madu the houseboy would say 'Memsahib the writer-wallah needs much quiet' no matter what arguments were in the air everyone would wander off and find something to do.

The smell of musk came through the open windows, small dark children played in the square below. Sounds from other flats echoed along the hallways.

Just before sunset I'd drive my children to the turf club grounds and while they trotted around on their ponies I'd walk Happy, our golden-red retriever.

I'd also walk him in the grounds of Prem Milan, where we lived and going down in the lift I became aware of a constant companion. A tall, fair man who looked gentle but aloof. Standing with his black cocker spaniel waiting to have its run. He was in fact a neighbour whose front door faced mine. He was also the 3rd Secretary at the Russian Embassy. His name was Colonel T. with a lovely Russian 'ski' at the end of it. He spoke to all the servants in the apartment block in Hindi and one of my servants said he would stop them on the backstairs and talk red-propaganda to them. There were no servants in his flat only a girl who came in every day to help and then went home. His large boned Russian wife spoke to no one.

In the tropic night with the moon glowing down on us as the dogs roamed around our legs the atmosphere tuned into the romantic, but only unsung Russian love-songs sprang from his eyes as I felt an odd feeling of the intelligentsia bugging my flat and the K.G.B. whisking me away in the black of night to some desolate outpost of Siberia, while the Russian Colonel brainwashed my children while my poor husband, after a day, long and hot in the High Courts slept through it all.

Outside the street doors of Hindu homes swamis* would sit on the ground waiting to be fed by a devout widow. Inside friends would talk of the Gita and Upanishads and everyone would become Hindi theologians for a fraction of a second. As the poems and epics and Vedic prayers too soon, became the deep, dark mysterious tunnel of Hindu mythology. It may suddenly show you a vision of eternity then send you back hurtling through Time to land on a bleak Indian plain where the burning sun obliterates the godhead. The teachings become obscure and worship becomes a question of traditions and a celebration of ritual offerings.

One of my favourite families were Muslim Khojas. They are an Ismaili sect and the Aga Khan is their spiritual head. They believe they have a direct descent from Mohammed. The orthodox of any religion are difficult if not impossible to know, but the educated are worldly and outgoing in their approach to Europeans.

The Khoja family were hospitable and responsive. They reminded me of a large noisy Mediterranean family with too many daughters, who were always being married off. And sons who refused to work and had gambling debts all over town.

A fat indulgent mother who had 'praise be to Allah' buried three husbands and one of the few homes in Bombay, where a scruffy mongrel could be seen scratching away under the table. They ate huge dishes of curried meats and fried onions were tossed over lamb kebabs. The mother sat at the head of a long table saying rude things about Hindus and Indian Jews with a twinkle in her narrow eyes, but a sarcastic lilt in her voice. She mumbled a Muslim grace in thanks for the food and everyone waited for the bearer to bring in the sherbet drinks and ice-cream.

Hamida, one of the unmarried daughters, showed me her jewels. With an 'open sesame' her room, became an Aladdin's cave, as she pushed the lid of a red-velvet jewel-case up,

*Swamis — Hindu Priests & Holy Men

the lid sprang back and sets of diamond rings and bangles lay
on satin pads along with collar necklaces studded with precious stones. They collect diamonds and bars of gold like we
collect sea-shells.

Many cultures have touched my life. Many gods have
shown me their painted faces. But I believe with my stubborn
heart in God The Almighty Father and hope He has a sense
of humour.

THE BAZAAR

A Bombay bazaar. The sun blazing down on a narrow street, where Indians rub against each other. Some buying, some selling, others begging, some stealing. All shouting, all too hot for the constant outbursts of words.

The bangle-seller offering dozens of glass or plastic bangles in a dazzle of bright colours. From a tray strapped to his thin waist, he cries his wares; at the top of a high pitched voice. And as he moves the glass bangles tinkle.

Everyone wants to sell me something. A monkey, a parrot, even a snake long and evil enough to make me shudder. Hot curry, smelling of onions and spiced meat bought for a few nai-paise and cold slices of pineapple splashed with running water to keep the flies off. And water melon with huge red pips and thick green skin.

A sikh wants to tell my fortune and a thin boy with misshapen legs and a withered hand begs, trying to beat the sun, his poverty and the passing cars' fast wheels.

Side-shops filled with saris and rolls of silk and cotton fabrics to fill a ship's cabin trunk to the brim. Brass that catches the glints of sunlight shows off the same pattern craftsmen used centuries ago.

Buffalo carts, clumsy and smelly are driven through the crowds by drivers who sit crossed-legged and chew betel nut. A small girl in a corner does a handstand for me and her brother does tricks. A balloon-wallah lets the breeze show off his wares as the balloons float above his head.

A dark skinned people mingle together with colour and movement. They are the pulse-beat of the Great Mother's heart, without which, she would die.

Here and there, white hippies, on their drug trail from the

cities of Europe and America sit yogi-fashion on the dirty ground. Desolate white beggars taken by the Great Mother for she never forsakes anyone. The pathetic outcastes have no place, even the Untouchables have a dignity of place and person beyond these Western drop-outs. For awhile the bazaar hides their shame and even drug illusion has its reality. The drugged eyes watch the dancing devils ready to plunge a dagger of despair into their vapid breasts.

The noise becomes impossibly loud. Indians shouting and haggling over every rupee. I thought their hands and heads would fall off from so much shaking back and forth. A shop-keeper gave me a coco-cola. I drank it through a suspect looking straw, convinced that a deadly plague would get me, before I reached the end of the bottle. My head began to spin from too much heat and noise. Urchins tried to hustle me into buying combs and safety pins. Pathetic bits and pieces they try to earn a day's food with. I could not resist the lovely dark eyes and ended up with enough combs and pins to last a life-time.

I struggled back to my car feeling exhausted telling the children to go away. A boy cleaning the windscreen, another waiting to open the door for me, all wanting money, all needing real work and understanding above my hand-out of small change.

Suddenly from an afternoon's carefree shopping all the problems of the Sub-Continent seemed to rest on my shoulders. Too much humanity, too much heat, too many flies and mosquitoes and too little human love beneath a burning sky.

I left the bazaar. The traders selling and shouting, their moving hands and chiselled faces. Masses of sandals strung agaist a wall. Pots and pans and statues of Krishna the Cow-boy and Indra riding his elephant.

I left them and drove slowly back to my apartment over-looking the Arabian sea and I wondered what it must be like being one of them. Eating spiced food, wearing chapples* and throwing petals and fruit offerings to their gods. The joss-sticks burn on altars placed before Lord Shiva God of creation, his work has been well done in this city off millions. But who is the god of salvation in Indian bazaars?

*Chapples — Flat sandals

WANDERERS UNDER THE SUN

Six hundred and fifty million people call the Sub-Continent country and mother. Bombay seems to be a foster-mother to many of them as her streets bulge with men, women and children. Because the street life is such an active force of movement and sounds. I often pinched myself into the fact that some of these beings lived in houses and apartments. Not everyone was a street dweller.

From this swell of walking flesh, dialects and languages are heard, as a song of speech. Gujarati, Urdu, Sindhi, Hindi, Marathi and even Tamil from the South of India. A beat of oriental voices high and low, soft and loud. Voices that have come down from a strange and mystic eastern past.

Only the sage is silent. The deaf and dumb gurgle sounds of misery as they beg, but the sage has brought his silence as a gift offering to the gods. The thin, long haired holy man walks the way of wise men. Outside of place and time completely self-contained and detached. His secrets burn behind his eyes. His mind of pure abstract thought patterns, has broken through the realms of his body and found its place with the stars.

Not for him the starched white trousers of the young men about town or the thin dhoti or white shirt and western suit. Not for him the arranged marriage. The family life programmed with computer-like perfection. Not for him the negative figure of an Indian husband in the matriarch society.

Our holy man is wise beyond the moon's rim and his eyes can see the message written on the pages of living souls. Illusions or delusion are for him Maya*, neither one, nor the other can trap his mind into the emotional demands of a

Maya — Delusion or illusion

fickle body.

He is untainted by the passing fancy of life's odd dream. It is almost absurd to think this holy creature was born of woman. No womb gave shelter to this being, who with a touch of his slender finger, felt the bodies of the gods.

This holy man came out of an egg. Just as Brahama emerged from his egg at the end of a thousand years, so the wise man of Bombay was hatched in the tradition of the golden egg the 'hiranyagarbha'. His mind is the Cosmic Mind. His unity with heaven breathes through his brain. He feels no fear. Not even the dreaded Kali Ma, the black mother, shakes his calm. The heat of the day and the cool of the night hold for him a thread that binds him to everlasting creation and makes of him a woven hope.

The undernourished weep at his feet, for a miracle. In their eyes he is a saint. But in the image of himself again and again he is re-absorbed into Hindu law until he is a part of the perfection of the holy river waters he is moving towards.

In the order of all things he will move towards the God-place of his pre-destination. His eyes will look up to the hills. His soul hold a memory of the forests of India at its creation. He is a Hindu, so there is no urgency in his walk towards eternity. No outward sign of action. He has his place with the gods and it will be there, when he arrives.

When his long walk comes to an end, he will lie his body down and close his eyes by the side of the burning ghat*.

A distant vision of the banyan tree will be his. India has always been the banyan tree with its huge aerial branches, its life giving shade. Its personification of motherhood with red figs for eating in time of famine.

The keeper of the burning ghat ignites the wand. The funeral pyre flames around a scented pile of sandal-wood joss-sticks. A bamboo flute can be heard from across the river banks. Tiny birds flutter above the curling smoke. Incense rises to the gods with a prayer held between the pale rays of smoke.

And so the wise man of the East ends his long walk far from the overcrowded streets of the Fair Bay. His soul has been released to find oblivion. In his final reward there is no re-birth cycle. On the banks of the Ganges his frail body

Ghat — stairway or range of hills

became ashes and found Paradise, Moksha, Nirvana or what you will.

In nearly every Hindu male, there is a yearning and a longing to become simply desireless of things of the world that seem mere glitter. He aches to leave everyone behind and take his life into the Great Thar, the Indian desert and give his tomorrows to his gods. The vultures do not bother him for they consume only the remains of Parsis*. He does not love his family less or more, but the need is to be alone under the sky of a Hindu heaven, where his spirit will dwell in the sun.

*The Parsi — dead are left for vultures in the Towers of Silence.

I'LL BET YOU FIFTY CHIPS

For the thrill of a dead-cert gamble, an Indian will bet his life away to the last inch of his jet-black hair. The Orient is a gamble-madhouse and money is won and lost to an alarming amount. Anything that has the chance of speed, the air of luck about it, will be worth a bet. Many a man in Bombay is the worry of his family because he is a compulsive gambler. Horses, numbers racket, dogs and even cockerels and racing cockroaches will all have bets placed upon their unlikely backs.

Servants will bet with eggs from the kitchens if they are low on funds and village land is won and lost to the tears of endless wives.

But, for good fun, there is a certain charm in listening to the punters, who are always going to win the next race or play the next ace. A lakh* of rupees will be won on the next throw of dice and chips are won and lost amid shouts of laughter.

When Lord Willingdon was Governor of Bombay in 1913 he founded the Willingdon Club. The club in Clerk Road is close by the Turf Club and the race-course.

Wealthy Indians and Europeans mingle with ease. They can be found playing polo, tennis or swimming in the turquoise pools, usually along with nubile Parsi girls or blonde American wives whose husbands are playing golf. The restaurant is a blaze of flowers and tables set with lush eastern dishes waiting to be eaten. A piece of contrived luxury under Bombay skies. Long glasses of iced coffee are sipped through pale pink straws as Bombay is a 'dry state' with strict prohibition laws, which means no beer or spirits to be seen,

*The Lakh is a hundred-thousand rupees

where Indians gather outside their homes.

About six in the morning during the racing season some fabulous horses can be seen on the early morning gallops. And, just before sunset, small children come for riding lessons, while mothers walk the dogs. Young lovers stroll around the course relaxed and happy in an atmosphere heavy with the scent of flowers. Elegant gladioli and a mass of tropical ferns give out a message of pleasure. Everyone who is anyone usually goes to the races on Sundays. The well-groomed rich men who win and lose fortunes and the women keeping their eyes on who is there and who isn't, as their saris sway and swing in the warm breeze. They look like flowers as they wave their diamond encrusted hands to greet their friends.

The city of the common-people, the Vaisyas, is far from this modern scene around the Turf Club, with its touch of Hollywood splendour. Or the Willingdon Club, where dim voices from the British Raj still echo in quiet rooms. The Great Mother, Fair Bay of the gods of the sea, there is hardly a trace.

A rather gloomy portrait of Gandhi-Ji hangs in a large room and his eyes look down on businessmen eating over-rich food. So far from his villages and hand-woven cloth and spinning-wheels are these wealthy philistines.

The social conscience he died for has lost its meaning. A servant in a white uniform comes to dust the marble floor. The whole puzzle of rich and poor is swept away with a grass whisk, as the servant bows his head and leaves the room. Where it may end, what sudden revolution will spill blood into overcrowded streets — who can tell?

The rich of India take the poverty for granted. But where families squat in pipes and the poor bend their heads in submission to Caste, one day these non-violent creatures may learn to demand more than a mission father's charity of faith and hope or a rich man's pavement hand-out.

THE FABULOUS SNAKES

Traveller pass through the jungle with care. You may see untouched jungle spaces, they have been left by devout believers in the cult-worship of The Nagas, a race of fabulous underworld serpents. The jungle clearing is to ask for a safe journey for humans, to spare them from the deadly fangs, the tortuous strangulation, swift and ruthless grasp of the snake.

South Indians especially believe reptiles to be gifted with amazing powers and place Nagas statues under trees and these shrines are worshipped in a highly symbolical and metaphysical sense.

Takshaka is a snake-king of great powers. His underworld capital is a glorious snake-kingdom of palaces and temples, where Takshaka and his Nagini queen receive the homage and chanted hymns of earthly devotees.

Nagas sometimes covet human possessions to enjoy in their own kingdoms and they come in human form to plunder what ever has caught their eyes, from an unsuspecting victim.

Great Indian dynasties claim with a strange pride Nagas among their royal ancestors and in a time of Cosmic peace, Vishnu sleeps under the protection of the snake-god Sesha. His seven heads raised to give the god shade. If thwarted, their surprise and trickery is fatal to humans and their's is a limitless world, where the giant spiders spin their snake-skin garments and copper insects hang from the breasts of their queens, as their snake bodies writhe and twist to the beat of the dark forest's sacred music.

They have a direct honesty. They poison and kill and make you aware of their powers as they say, 'Do not conspire against us O humans, because we are honest, but let us rule our underworld kingdoms as we choose. Ours is the venom of mystic healing! We declare war only on those who stumble without care on our jungle clearings'. So travellers the warning is yours to obey. Go in peace along the highway of fabulous snakes. But beware, King Takshaka may covet your treasures and the thunders of the underworld will darken the skies, as he bears down his demands upon your smooth shoulders.

Pass by the tree statues with a polite nod to the gods and praise the snake-charmer in the hot bazaar. Give alms to wandering monks. Do not damage the wings of a butterfly. And water plants and trees. Offer nuts to monkeys and show respect for the strength of the tiger.

For in jungle groves, as you wander through this land; the Nagas powerful and dangerous, may take the shape of a humble beggar. And if you have not paid tribute to the animals, fruits and plants of India, his eyes will wound you and your soul will evaporate into the jungle mists.

THE AYAH

She was enormously fat. As she walked her great buttocks rolled from one side of her hips to the other. She was very black and her round face pocked marked and wrinkled, almost like a monkey in her expressions, clearly showed her Dravidian ancestry.

The skin and face of one, whose beginnings went far back in time to the dark forests and to the birth of the very gods themselves.

Her fat arms were tattooed with blue crosses, the sign of being a Christian convert in a Hindu country.

When she smiled her teeth and tongue almost frightened me out of my wits till I grew to love her, as they were bright scarlet from too much pan and betel nut chewing. Her hands were work-worn, yet so gentle and her eyes sparkled with village humour and also untold depths of sadness.

Her broken English told me a few things about her way of life, before she came to Bombay to be an ayah. The husband who used to beat her, when he drank village liquor. The village near Madras, where her children were born and the way she worked in the city to send money back home for them. So they would not starve and chew betel nut all day to forget hunger pains or have only rice-water to drink.

Yes, she missed them, but she was a servant, but her 'Jesus' would take care of them, while she took care of my children.

When she was over-excited she broke into her native Tamil, a language not spoken in Bombay and her huge body shook with whatever emotion she felt. Perhaps anger or laughter.

She had the wisdom of the peasant, neither able to read or write, but somehow wise to worldly things and compassionate and kind, as they are, who have suffered.

The letter-writer sitting under a black umbrella to keep the sun off his head would write her letters for her. Once a month she would walk to the corner of the road, where he worked and tell him her newsletter for her family. Then it would be posted off and when the reply came back he would read it to her, in Tamil. Having great respect for the written word, she admired the letter-writer for being literate.

She would stand for hours in the hot, steamy afternoon, ironing the tropical cottons and piles of children's clothes, sometimes muttering to herself maybe a prayer or more likely a curse. Who knows the mutterings of servants, when the day is hot and the work seems endless. She would croon to herself chants that came from the core of India. From the jungle trees twisted with snakes. From the hills and valleys and rivers. The chants would call India, India and with her eyes half closed, she saw a vision of forests and ancient fires and gods leaping from the flames for the first time coming into existence with all their glory.

She would sit sewing with her fat legs crossed or eating curries that were hot and spicy as the devil's fangs, with her hands.

My children adored her. She spoiled them hopelessly. Never cross, always ready to cuddle and comfort a weeping little boy or a vexed daughter who was late for school or a ballet lesson.

Her methods knew nothing about child discipline or modern thoughts on how children should be brought up. The child to her was a symbol of woman's fertility. The child was adored, because the child was creation.

She washed her long black hair and let it hang down her broad back to dry in the morning sun and without the oiled bun, tightly drawn to the nape of her neck, she looked very feminine. I wondered where her youth had gone and how she had grown fat and ugly.

Knowing the brutal side of village life, where women with despair drown themselves in the village wells, her survival was a miracle.

She would say she was a hundred years old, when the children asked her age and, as she had little idea of birthdates, she must have seemed very old. She was often silent. Solitude came without effort to her. She rarely went out and would wander about the apartment with her cotton sari trailing on the marble floors. Her bare feet black as night skies against the white tiles.

For me she became the flag of those who have no rights. She was a servant there to work and, if she worked badly, to be dismissed. In my home this did not apply, but in India, where servants come and go, not as people, but as hands, that clean and wash and sweep and serve.

She was Liberty crying behind the skirts of the rich. She was education aching to be taught and brought to millions who know slavery in overcrowded countries. She was Freedom burning to escape and know the meaning of the passport and birth certificate.

As she worked and took care of my children she was completely unaware of the struggle she represented. I wonder what will happen when the day of reckoning dawns in overcrowded lands!

THE DAY THAT THE RAINS CAME DOWN

May, the month of delicate spring flowers in Europe. May is Grishma in Bombay, the hot season. When the plains of India become hotter and hotter until even the mosquitoes die from too much heat, half way to biting me to bits.

Air-conditioners go on full blast. The city has become a living oven. The birds seem too hot to fly and everyone is slightly irritable. Families drive off to the hills, the law-courts are closed and the delicious mango makes up for it all by coming just in time. Eaten with pleasure or drunk from tall glasses as its pulp is liquidized and iced. The whole month of May is a humid experience of sticky perspiration and damp clothes and clammy nights.

Then near to June, when it all seems too much to bear, distant rumbles are heard from the sky. Thunder and streaks of scarlet lightning cross the darkening clouds. Once so vivid a blue now a sky with a tone of grey, as the thunder becomes louder and nearer the city.

Carpenters strengthen window-shutters for the owners of large houses that are built by the sea shore. The wind gains power and blows anything and everything, everywhere.

Palm trees wave and stoop in the strong breeze. The sea looks grim, and after about three weeks of these signs from above, the first drops of rain fall on an overheated Fair Bay. The annual rains have come. The monsoon has broken.

Hymns to Indra the great god of rain have been answered. Indra has thundered from his eternal reign in the tropical skies and he has let loose the rains onto the needy red soil below. Indra, the noble god and lord of heaven received the prayers of his people and blessed the rains. Riding his elephant Airavata, who was born from the sea of milk, Indra triumphs in the storm and everyone in Bombay runs for cover.

Huge waves splash their foamy spray over passing cars on Marine Drive. The hems of saris get soggy. Umbrellas go up. Floods turn side streets into small canals. Indra is praised. Mosquitoes vanish for awhile. They lay their eggs in the swamps and swarms of black flies take their place.

The sky is a dramatic show of fantastic thunder and I can almost believe the gods had a lot to do with it.

Most English people have heard about Lands End, Cornwall, England, but few know about Lands End, Bombay. Tucked away behind some of the beautiful eastern houses including the Governors residence and blocks of modern flats.

Lands End seems to be the end of everything, for there is only sea and rock, not even a grain of sand, but great lumpy pebbles, black and grey and slippery. The rocks are massed together and form a small island against the sea, but not in it. In the early morning before the sun is fierce, Lands End is near to paradise.

Clothes are brief. Its very quiet and tiny fish glitter in the rock pools. Everything is warm and the sea smells of the tropics. Strange birds dive into the waves for food. Dogs spring in and out of the water as pieces of banana leaves float like canoes on top of the green foam.

Soon the dhobi* will come with the washing cleaned and already to be laid on the high rocks to dry, because he handles soiled clothes and linen, he is an Untouchable, but Caste seems of no importance here, on a fine morning, by the strong rocks.

The odd dreamer will come and gaze and smoke a cigarette or throw stones into the waves and wander on.

Few come here. Only the dreamers and the idle and me, who is perhaps a mixture of both these contemplative joys. Those in love might find the sea too abrupt for their happiness to touch it. But I adore the miles of nothingness and the desolate fishing boats that sail by.

The rocks are dangerous and wet feet are cut and bruised, trying to reach the water's edge. But because it's warm it does

*Dhobi — Laundryman

not matter. As my hands held on to the rocks, I could feel the strength of centuries of Indian life burned into their hardness.

Just before dark, as the sun drifts into the sea and the moon comes out, the moon they call 'the home of the dead', the rocks look proud and aloof. Their kingdom is unknown. They have seen Time and Place and The Everlasting all come from the sea and no humans will conquer their might.

I dared to walk to Lands End, as the monsoon raged and I was too terrified to move. Waves taller than ships beat against the rocks. Rain fell from the sky in a kind of tropical madness.

Indra was supreme. The birds howl and the wind shakes the life-force out of the sea. One battle of rain, sea and wind. The palms bending with exhaustion and pebbles piled up into black heaps, where the wind has pushed and left them.

On such days no washing is left to dry. No passer-by stops to stare. Only birds fight the storm as the rocks stand like giants holding their heads high to honour Indra, god of the storm.

The fish and crabs retreat. I miss their bright, quick beauty. The windows of the houses and flats are protected with nailed shutters and Lands End is left alone until the rains have ended and a shimmer of a rainbow is glimpsed in the sky.

Then once more the days shall be quiet and warmth will guide my footsteps along the slippery road to gaze at the Arabian sea and fondle black pebbles in my hand.

BRIGHT RING OF GREEN

Bombay city of sandals, city of green-winged parakeets as green as the lush grass grown overnight, from the fresh rains. Grown in an instant. A flash of new creation. Everywhere a new vision, a new colour to the old city.

The rains have ended and great pujas* of adoration go to the goddess Parbhati, Siva's wife, who wears a crescent moon in her hair.

Footsteps linger from the past. Eight hundred years of Muslim rule is tossed aside, broken and parted into another country.

The holy Koran moved on. Leaving a fragment of Muslims living in quiet dignity in the ancient quarters of the city.

After their harsh fast of Ramadan, begun in the deep heat before the rains, then relief from the overcrowded mosques. Irritable faithful of Islam, worn out with their rituals, bless the rains. The Imam leading the prayers of devout slaves of Mohammed. The rhythmic prayers echo a chant of past violence against Hindus. And then at last the rains come and go.

The moon touching the minarettes. Deserted ablution tanks, where the faithful cleanse their faces and necks, wait for the former masters of India, beneath a dark sky.

The capricious Hindu gods keep a friendly eye on the devotions directed towards Mecca, as Muslim women, deeply shrouded in black purda, wail their prayers kneeling on thin prayer mats.

Bombay is a Hindu city. Yet Islam's rule lingers. With Muslim poetry and music, crafts and delicious cooking. This polyglot city embraces the charms as well as the problems.

*Pujas — Prayers and offerings to the Gods

Veiled women and dream-like men who play Indian classical music on weird and wonderful instruments. There is an unspoken rift as religion inflicts a pain upon the races.

The rains have left the city cool and they are weak with fasting. It is enough that life's harsh tests end at the appointed time. Islam came and conquered. Built Mosques and palaces fit for their Empire's kings. And left a weave of fairytales along the edges of their history. The grass is fresh and gentle voices called Bhai to each other, brother, brother and the gods look down on the rain-softened red earth.

A green city waits the return of the lawyers and their plain wives, now the courts are sitting again. They come back from the hills to a rather corrupt system of bribes and disorder. It seems hard to believe, there may be propriety and order in the court-actions, that to a European seem very shady indeed.

For a few rupees I was shown around the courts and told how they work by the guide, as rogue after rogue came before the judges.

Asia must be taken on trust, that all in the end will be well. And it's best not to be involved with law.

After the rains the Fair Bay is still rather wet, still plagued with flies. A flock of goats push and bleat along the road as a sandal-maker sits outside his shop stitching leather sandals. Ready to be hung in bundles over the doorway.

The high-born Hindus, say, he will be banished to Naraka, the Hindu hell, because he handles cow-hide. But he believes the gods are kind to him, even in his low Caste state, because his family is fed everyday. So he accepts banishment to hell with humility and paints red and gold patterns on the strips of black leather.

All meet in death, say the Parsi sages. Rich and poor, high born and low born take their places together before the throne of judgement.

Parsis fled from Muslim persecution in Persia about 2,000 years ago. They believe all life is sacred and must not be defiled by a corpse. Earth and air, fire and water are sacred and the dead must not come into contact with this holiness.

They make their dead offerings to vultures. Amid beautiful gardens stand the Five Towers of Silence, on Malabar Hill. I always shudder when passing Malabar, thinking about the dead being fed to the waiting birds of prey. A macabre place, even if the gardens are exquisite. It has a Dracula-like omen about it and Hindus joke the Parsis live to be very old, because they are scared stiff of dying and going to the vultures.

As the vultures turn their cold eyes away from the white bones, the owners of the luxury houses on the hill must dislike the Towers of Silence being on their doorsteps with the reminder that all meet in death as the eternal flame of the Parsi faith burns in the silent gardens of the dead.

The traveller wanders in a strange world, but the way of the prophet Zoroaster must be observed from generation to generation. He kindled the sacred fire the Parsis worship in the 6th century B.C. and the Parsi Faith began. God is in everything on earth and fireworship is His symbol.

The litter being carried through the streets holding a sect-marked Hindu corpse, followed by a wailing group of women wearing saffron robes and scattering marigolds, seems a purer way of death to me.

Better think of dining with Parsi friends than of their funeral-rites. They have very western style homes and may offer for dinner a well-flavoured palla fish, which is rather like a salmon. They are at home with Europeans, but very often a Hindu household is like Fort Knox to the 'unclean' British.

Parsi financiers have given much to Bombay. Charitable foundations abound with famous Parsi names. They admired the Raj and their women wear western clothes with chic and many have very fair skins.

But the core is eastern. The fruit charitable to its own kith and kin. Remote from Hindu and Muslim, they live in a world of their own. On the surface of everyday living all communities float above each others lives. The sun shines down on everyone. This city that takes them all to her breast, like a huge warm parent, is at times mother to a storm of discontent, which breaks like a thunderbolt from the blue. Old wounds open and the drums of salvation beat out a warning, as people shut their doors and others walk quickly by.

To love ones neighbour belongs to another faith and so the communities touch in reality and part in spirit. Mahatma

Gandhi lives his ideal of total assimilation of all Castes and creeds. But although Bapuji's picture hangs with other saints on the walls of Hindu homes, garlanded with flowers. His message lies on the sands of Chaupati beach, where he talked to his people.

The sea flows back and forth over his rhetoric. The social conscience he fought for has failed. As fly-overs leap above Marine Drive erected by poverty stricken workers no better than slaves. Time marches on and his message lies at the Untouchables feet, a damaged and lost ideal.

'GAJANANA' ELEPHANT FACE

The ascetic Brahmins in the religion of their Lord and Master Siva, give praise to my own special and favourite god, Ganesa,* the elephant-god. When I was a little girl I always wanted a present of a baby elephant and used to think countries like Thailand admirable, because they held the elephant to be a supreme creature.

After the rains, when the streets are still moist, images of Ganesa made of clay and brightly painted are paraded through the streets. It is a laughing, happy festival and the Great Mother still sprouts fresh green grass from the red earth.

The goddess Parvati made the elephant-god from the dew of her body mingled with dust and he acts as a guardian to the goddess's gate. In a fit of wild temper Siva cut off the head of Ganesa, because he tried to prevent the Lord and Master from entering through the gate to Parvati's chambers. But then Siva felt sorry for his fury and said Ganesa should be given a new head of the first animal that walked by the gate. The first animal, which happened to come along was an elephant and Parvati's guardian of the gate had a new appearance. They called him, 'Gajanana' elephant-face.

He is small and stocky with four arms and a fat belly, because he can be a bit of a glutton. He carries an alms bowl, an elephant-goad and prayer-beads. And he rides a rat.

When they were out together riding across the sky a snake frightened the rat and the elephant-god fell to the earth with a violent bump and burst his fat stomach.

Ganesa rolled the snake around his damaged belly until the snake healed him and the moon laughed and jeered at the

*Ganesa — also this Hindu deity is known as Ganesh

d

god's accident.

In a rage Ganesa broke off one of his tusks and threw it in the moon's face which until this day periodically denies the moon of light. The curse lingers and Hindus are prohibited from looking at the moon on the day of Ganesa's festival and if by chance they should see it they get a neighbour to abuse them so the curse may be removed.

I always fill his alms bowl with special fruits, because he is also the god and patron of literature. His nature is of two intelligent beings, man and elephant. He loves humanity and humanity loves him. He is gentle, calm, propitious and full of good sense, charm and friendliness. He bestows riches and success. Before all other gods he is honoured first. And even today if a bank fails in Bombay they turn the statues of Ganesa to face the wall and clients know what has happened!

My children when they were small and visited zoos always took a bag of iced buns for the elephants. A gift from me to Ganesa's earth-bound brothers and sisters.

UP TO THE HILLS AND FARAWAY

Once again the plains are dry and hot. The grass has faded and the masses walk the streets searching for a Hindu saint.

Come with me driving along one of the only two roads out of Bombay. It is time to leave the city for awhile. To get up and go, up to the hills and faraway. The drive is hot and dusty to begin with. Congested roads and heavy lorries do not make for easy tempers, when the sun beats down. But with patience and learning the neat tricks of weaving the car in and around buffalo carts, donkeys, goats and dogs, old lame men and children, the journey will take shape.

Village after village passes by. Not too far from Bombay a stench of fish drying in the sunshine overpowers the nostrils and I was glad to drive through this fishing village, hardly aware of the fishermen and their way of life. The smell was too much for me. On and on, into and out of drab villages, where Gandhi's dream of a better India stabs the heart.

To unaccustomed eyes the poverty is always a shock. Children covered with flies and sores making balls of dung to burn for cooking fuel. Pregnant women carrying water-pitchers on their heads as the men drink tea in tea-houses. Crows fighting chickens for droppings. Pecking at hard baked soil that yields almost nothing nutritious. Starving cows, a patch of green grass and girls working the paddy-fields. Maybe a temple for village worship of the phallic god Lord Siva god of fertility. A modern garage and usual beggars the second the car stops to re-fuel.

It almost seemed wrong to go to the hills. But my driver shrugged it off with a grin and asked me how many babies I wanted to take with us. I wished I could have given them all a better life. But their idea of poverty is not like mine. They are used to so little and rarely ask for more.

The car headed for Poona and lunch. Poona, the very name brings images of old British colonels writing to *The Times* and signing themselves 'Disgusted'.

Then after many a hot Indian mile the magnificent Western Ghats come into sight. The pathway to the hills. Before the climb up the Ghats can begin, an offering is made to the gods. I placed my coins before the shrine not wishing to offend the smiling god, only the brave would avoid this superstition as the Ghats can be deadly.

The car begins to pull and chug. We climb higher and higher. My driver prays the wheels won't go into a skid. My Ayah holding my small son as if the end of the world was nigh and my daughter feeling car-sick.

I gazed in a dream at the scenery. Too awe-inspiring to believe it was real. I had no doubts about the car being safe, after all I had put 30 rupees into the god's lap and he could not possibly want more to get us all to the top safe and well.

The sky was blue and full of promise. The hills and valleys seemed to glow with sweet, cool air. The hot plains were forgotten. The ugly villages vanished. Only Mahabaleshwar the hill-station, lovely, lovely sight. 4,421 ft. above sea level to a realm of delight. A lake with tiny boats and groups of women chatting together and chewing nuts. Small ponies pulling red painted gigs. Honeymooners from Bombay looking lovesick and very few people but the local inhabitants, as I had brought my family out of season.

Brown wooden bungalows with large gardens, heaps of donkeys and chirping birds of paradise showing off their feathers. Where had the Great Mother with her struggle for survival gone? Where were the teeming crowds? Here was only the Krishna Valley and The Blue Valley and Hunter's Point and Connaught Ride. All very British names. The Raj was here in the regal past.

Sudden darkness reminded me it was still India. The quick sinking of the sun and the moon and stars as always. The shrieks of the wild animals and the giant moths flying against the lamps in my bedroom. As queer looking bats fly through the night and the air is heavy with jasmine and the servants bring my children iced-drinks. A deep tropical tiredness made my eyes heavy and I fell asleep high up in the hills of India. Early morning and long walks breathing fresh air, buying bananas and feeding the ponies. A visit to Old Mahabaleshwar and a stop at the sacred temple then buying orchids and walking around the Chinese Gardens. The waterfalls captured a part of me forever. The Falls of Jenna fall into a lake 1,000 ft below.

The local people dress in bright costumes. The girls wear silver trinkets all over their bodies and some of the hill tribes can be seen stark naked climbing up and down the green banks like shy, swift animals.

With thoughts of England, Arthur's seat had to be seen and with all the legends about King Arthur, I suddenly realised it must have been India, where he lived out all his passions, after all, where else could it have been?

In the afternoons merchants came to my bungalow to sell me arts and crafts, books and toys. The sandal-maker came to take orders for soft leather chappals that would be stitched and ready to wear by evening.

The fruit-seller came with baskets of ripe strawberries fresh from the strawberry gardens and arranged on layers of rose-leaves with tiny pink rose-buds tucked inside the green leaves, like a fragile poem without words. Almost as if a lover had arranged them so, for a very special lady.

Time could stand still and this second would remain a memory of sweet pictures floating on clouds. The hills beckon romance and lie in wait to catch an unsuspecting heart.

A panther or tiger may jump over the car and snakes hiss in the undergrowth. Through the narrow spaces between the Ghats, the Konkan coast can be seen. The sea is there, but the air is usually heavy with mists.

Walking and talking and exploring had to come to an end. With regret and surprise that our holiday was over. I felt like a child filled with yearning, because it all ended so soon. Back in the car, the long, long drive down the Ghats began. Back to Mumbai* and the dusty plains. But I will return and find paradise again. The coolie-paths and Dhobi Waterfalls and temples and small children pulling giant butterflies along on pieces of string shall be mine once more.

*Mumbai — vernacular — Bombay

PRINCES, PIRATES, SAILORS and WHORES

On The Apollo Bunder the sailors from around the world unite. Wisecracking that Bombay can be smelled seven miles away from port. The Fair Bay has a perfect natural harbour and the fleets come and go. White P&O liners either homeward or outward bound show their flags. The American fleet is in and that means dollars to spend.

White-hippies hitching from the drug spots laze about The Gateway of India. They are pathetic, chewing on sugar-cane sticks and scratching fleas in their hair picked up on the drug-trail from Afghanistan. The hard drug cases hide away in seedy, nightmare rooms in back streets waiting for death to strike. The hashish smokers squat on the pavements talking with sailors, making dirty jokes about local prostitutes, dusky painted ladies of the town or French or Portuguese girls who can be procured at a price. There is always a dark little chap standing around offering you the delights of his brother and sister.

The hippies 'high' on sura, Indian booze made from fermented sap from the palm. The other jinx of the city is not so well known by Europeans, who fall under his spell in the tropics, is the hot-city demon also called Sura. He is a Hindu genie who will lead the vulnerable into every vice-trap and sin laden hovel in the East. Sura can also be a good angel, who like other Hindu gods will find a resting place in one's body, the head or fingers or palm of hand are favourite places, but it's best not to take chances after dark with any of the three Suras; they mean trouble!

Boys selling carved boxes from Kashmir laugh at hippies, point at their dirty, tanned skins and torn jeans and wonder what happened to the super-sahibs. Sura must have laid a curse on their blond heads.

Across the broad street the Taj hotel majestic and welcoming, catches the last beams of fading sunshine on its façade. A new Taj has been built next to it, but the old hotel is fit for a king.

And from one of the great States of Rajasthan a Maharaja is staying at the hotel. Coming to Bombay for a function or to visit friends. His bodyguard sits Indian fashion on the carpeted floor outside His Highnesses suite. A stern looking man with a sword at his hip, wearing a scarlet turban. Yet another page from the Arabian Nights unfolds its glamour. The Government of India may have taken the Privy Purses away from the Princes and divided their land into lots for the peasants to share, but the Princes remain a legend unto themselves. Holy leaders of their people. They are called 'The Children of The Fire Pit' Agnikula. They are romance and chivalry and famed warriors. Sadly, the heirs of some famous Princes have degenerated into Western type playboys, spoiled by wealth. But their aura has outlasted bad reputations and songs are sung to the glory that was Rajasthan. At heart the Fair Bay is a romantic and the Rajputs are greeted with a deep bow of respect. A king is a king is a king.

The night has a thousand eyes and the sinister night people leave their mark. The quick murder, the kidnapped child. Beaten and raped girls, corrupt police and informers, drug pushers and pimps.

The sleeping poor huddled in smelly groups on the sides of the streets are unaware of the evil in the night. Life for them anyway is a grotesque joke and their one luxury is sleep, so they sleep on.

Wailing Indian music comes from dark alleyways. The night people will fade with the coming dawn, to come out again with the black overblown rats and cockroaches and carrion crows.

The dance of existence moves to the beat of the drums. Hari Krishna is sung along the roads, as a group of travelling transvestites entertain the sailors. Dancing a mock village dance of welcome, with their long black hair and painted eyes offering sex, while their coloured saris blow in the sea breeze. Banging their effeminate fingers up and down on tambourines decorated with bright orange ribbons matching their hennaed finger-nails. They shout the names of the gods, dancing and singing and collecting money from bewildered looking sailors who think it's all a giggle.

The night shopping and whore hunting ends. The sailors return to their ships and the pirates of the city take their bounty to mysterious dwellings in dark parts of Bombay.

And so the first green parrot of morning spreads its wings as the brass-seller wipes the dust off his wares and the potter sets out hundreds of pots and cups, that are used just once by the Hindu pious, then thrown away as 'unclean'. The naked children who have never heard of school run about the back streets as the sun flames against posters of the latest Indian films. Sensual, heavily painted actors smile toothy grins at the passing crowds. The screen lovers will dance and sing their way through four or five hours of film epics. Telling of Indian wars and legends. Taking the cast over mountain ranges, flooded rivers, palaces and desolate hills and endless villages. The lovers will not kiss, but will wail in high Indian voices of their passion, feuds and families.

After these films the houseboys will live out their fantasies with a cheap visit to Bombay Cages, where prostitutes in cage-like windows stand on show. On Alakshmi Day, the lady of ill luck and goddess of prostitution, incense fires can be seen outside all brothels in India. The women are allowed to give no other offering to the Hindu gods.

Delicious smells come from a chinese restaurant and the owner plays mah-jongg, moving 144 pieces of the strange Chinese game, with hands that seem restless and eyes that never betray a single thought. Maybe they are spies from across the borders — who can tell?

Russian envoys drive past in sombre black cars looking clever and even more secretive than the Chinese. Waiting for the day the red flag will blow in the tropic breeze.

The Great Mother holds them all in her maternal lap. The people walking her streets are not really concerned about political subjugation that the great powers may be conspiring against them. The gods take care of their troubles. It is far wiser to eat curry and polish white ivory ornaments ready to be sold.

High noon sun is too fierce for arguments and let those who work get on with it quietly and without fuss.

Underneath a tree of perfect knowledge, an American sips a sweet-lime drink. It's very, very hot, but soon it will be winter, the season of Hemanta and then Shishira, the cold season. Bombay has her seasons and moods, but to the American tourist the tropics are always too hot and sticky.

A small black baby crawls towards its mother. She puts it to her breast and they fall asleep in the sun leaning against the red bricks of The Gateway of India. A history is cemented in these bricks, but she holds her baby and sleeps, history is not her problem.

BY THE LIGHT OF THE SILVERY MOON

Khandala is a beautiful village with a great awesome ravine and waterfall, about 80 miles from Bombay. On hot sticky Bombay nights as the hot season becomes more and more humid we would drive to Khandala for a week-end away. Either leaving early in the morning before the sun was after us or driving at night by the light of the moon. One year on my birthday an odd gathering of friends joined us for my bungalow-party. Like all parties some uninvited guests arrived with their own brand of jokes and humour. My motley collection of Indians and Bohemians from unknown European beginnings, laughed and lazed and danced and talked their way through a crazy week-end.

A Greek actress wearing a red wig, now middle-aged and the madam of a brothel was brought by a weird Englishman who was wearing a dhoti. I think someone had told them my party was for fancy-dress only. She had a pet cockerel and we all said her cook would dish it up for her one day in a chicken curry. She had little English and less Hindi and amid our laughter shouted, 'If cooki killi my cocki, I killi cooki'. Another exile played 'Blue Moon' for me on the old upright piano, which had mice nesting in it. A Parsi with bright blue eyes and a bored wife flirted with a French girl who claimed she had hitched from Afghanistan, but I think she flew in from Pondicherry. We were allowed drinking permits as we came from the West and as we sipped our 'scotch on the rocks' and the piano-player became a little drunk, the Greek sang homesick songs and I peeled the skins off huge black grapes and shoved them into everyone's mouths.

Within almost minutes of our arrival a villager came to the main door and handed the bearer a tatty prescription for penicillin. He needed the drug for his very sick wife. We all knew he wanted money for village liquor, but no one was in a mood to moralize so he was given the rupees.

Stories were told about twelve-year old girls being given to old men as brides. Child-brides are against the law, but it still happens. The village world can be a dark unknown place. There are thousands of villages, there is violence, child-brides, and terrible superstitious offering to the gods.

Back at my party a Muslim who drank only iced orange water was telling the exiles of the epic adventures of Ashoka and Akbar the great Islamic rulers. He ended by giving us a recitation of a moving Urdu poem. I did not understand a word, but wept with the others, pure, stroppy, whisky tropical tears.

Dogs barked, strange echoes came from the country-side. Moths flew into our faces and week-end hedonists that we were, we threatened to throw anyone into the ravine who mentioned politics, American Aid or problems they were having with their lovers or mistresses.

The men gambled with dice, while the women talked of new novels, Italian hairdressers now the rage in Bombay and their gynaecologists.

The air was pungent with wild Indian flowers and the dhoti-wearing Englishman was asking the Greek madam if it were true that powdered rhinoceros horn was an aphro-disiac. I didn't hear her reply as the pan-seller from the village came to sell the addicted the rolled leaf filled with betel-nut paste and pieces of real shredded gold or silver, meant to do wonders for the stomach. What with pan and powdered Rhino's horn I really expected any minute to see the fabled unicorn float down from the sky with a white body, dark red head and dark blue eyes. With a phallic horn of enormous strength in the centre of his forehead. I then expected this monster stallion to carry me off to wonderland.

Sadly I was told the unicorn was known only to cure epilepsy, when its horn was powdered down and taken in a potion. It was also an infallible remedy against any kind of poison. Alas, there wasn't a convulsion in sight only one of the servants rolling out chapattis in a corner of the kitchen.

By the light of the silvery moon my friends danced on the cool grass and we had kite battles before falling asleep on thick Indian floor rugs.

In the morning thousands of birds woke everyone up. We walked into the village waving my birthday balloons in the air like free, happy children. Congress Hindus wearing homespun khaddi cloth jackets and Nehru caps looked at us with dismay and quickly vanished to take a ritual bath after contact by sight with the 'unclean'.

My birthday antics over. All the balloons blown across the ravine. The paper kites tangled in the tree tops, my house-party friends waving goodbye from their car windows and the sun just beginning to be very hot.

A small black mouse from the piano ran across the pathway chased by a thin local cat. I closed the bungalow doors, told the servants to check the shutters and drove back to Bombay one year older.

SAFFRON, WHITE and GREEN

Thousands come by car, they come in buffalo carts, they walk, they run. They come on donkeys and bicycles. They bang drums to thank their gods. They blow whistles. They shout and sing and clap their hands. The cripples shuffle and hobble and everyone else dances through the laughing crowds.

The people of Maharashtra celebrate with almost divine joy August 15th.* Remembering with pride the gaining of Indian Independence in 1947.

The centre of Bombay becomes a carnival. The saffron, white and green Indian flag blows from windows and balconies and small children wave them about in the hot air.

Cars are decorated with saffron, green and white flowers. Women wear saffron coloured saris. The Great Mother has become a garland of moving, ecstatic Indians, waving their national flag before the world and shouting 'we are free'. They shout in many tongues, 'we may be poor, but we are free'.

Thus the Raj came and left its footprints on the Sub-Continent map. But as the saffron, white and green flag blows over the land, sea, mountains, forests and deserts that are India, it is good to remember with all the arguments for and against British rule, that many generations suffered. The young British soldiers sent out to help keep the peace for The Empress of India, Queen Victoria, often died in misery.

The European cemetery at Sewri holds the bones of men and women and children who died in the prime of life far from their own shores of foul illness. Dysentery, cholera, typhoid fever and smallpox carried them to early graves. And

*Independence Celebrations Jan. 26th

the troops were rotten with V.D. and consumption.

The remains of tiny Arrabella aged three years, of Marcus James aged five, of Mary Louise Smith aged twenty-two lie scattered and forgotten in red Indian soil. Victims of foreign policy. They followed their menfolk around the world and perished.

A few white memsahibs stayed after Independence. Now very old, they sip Hyson, a green Chinese tea and in retrospect talk of the days of Empire when the P & O liners brought the élite to the other side of Suez. Now emigrants on route to Australia shop round the Bombay emporiums and they would not be Empire builders for a queen's treasure.

As the flags of nations change and blow in the breeze. So the world in a continual state of flux, goes round.

The Gateway of India, erected for King George V and Queen Mary to walk under, when they landed in Bombay in 1911, stands as a reminder and a warning that the Raj came and relinquished its claim on The Land of Nod. Bara Sahibs, Chota Sahibs and Viceroys have washed their hands and gone into their own sweet land.

The Independence Day celebrations come to a hot and noisy climax with dinner served Hindu style. Large peaceful rooms with prized carpets hanging against cool walls, where green money-plants seem to be growing out of the ceiling.

A family horoscope-chart telling the joint family destiny is shown like a painting would be in the West. The usual prints of Krishna and Gandhi, and the women of the household wearing their saris wound clock-wise round their bodies the special way Gujarati women dress at home.

Someone telling the cook to hurry up in a loud voice and a chorus of 'Ach chaa', 'all right, all right'. Someone else calling for water to be brought to the table, 'pani, pani', to be drunk with a touch of sweet or sour lime added. Glass is unclean so pani is drunk from tall, silver goblets.

The extreme orthodox members of the family eat alone. No one but the cook must touch a morsel of their food. Placed before the diners is a brass thali. The lovely carved Indian dish, like a huge curved plate. The total meal is neatly served in heaps, appetizing and small, around the edges of the brass plate.

Milk, curds, ghi and buttermilk are prized even before rice and vegetables in these vegetarian homes, but rice and vegetables are mildly spiced and very tasty.

Small hot chapattis and delicate salads, piles of fruit and nuts. No cutlery of any kind. Cries of 'try this and this, le jao, le jao'. Hot bright red bananas add colour to the eastern feast underneath a purring fan. All spread out on a carved rose-wood table low on the ground. A delightful end to the day of tributes. As Hindus remember those who shed their blood so that the saffron, white and green flag could be raised over their ashes, sprinkled on the river waters of the Sub-Continent.

PASS BY PILGRIM, PASS BY

Holiness for me in India could not be found within the walls of Temples or Mosques. Holiness came with hot, rushing air. With the white foam on top of giant waves pushing the Arabian sea across the sands of the Fair Bay.

It came with feelings and smells and sights. With the humble sweeper in her torn sari. In the faces of the poor who know starvation is always near.

Holiness for me was not the bluff and thunder of the gods, but the moving river edged with palms. It was the Ghats and the grey goat tied up outside a shack ready to become a sacrifice at a Muslim festival.

Holiness is the way people live out their destinies without a grudge against humanity for being born and dying a whole life away on a railway-station platform. Holiness is the benign old man who asks for nothing and children's cheeks are touched with it, although covered with flies.

It comes in the night as the sky breaks out in a glitter of stars and it is the guest of pilgrims going their different ways towards the mansion in heaven with many rooms.

It is in the songs of eastern poems. In the talk of saints and fakir. It is in the offering from human beings to the Lord of all creation as they sit in hut or palace.

Holiness is the praise and passion of those who care. It is in the musical chime of flute and drum and tinkling bangles. An unbroken bond between the creation and the Lord.

It comes as a handmaiden to serve the saints and dwells at the feet of those who seek the company of God.

Pilgrims pass by on their way to Benares to do penance for their sins and to eat cow dung and drink cow urine before they are given absolution. As heads are shaved some will mock others weep. And lions will tread their way in the forests.

Lamas pass by in saffron robes, sweet smelling joss slowly burns as holiness becomes the perfect harmony of mind and body.

It is the beauty of the lotus flower, the fish, the lake, the mountain and it lies on the horizon's brim, where it waits to be reborn again and again.

For India Mahatma Gandhi cried love. Pandit Nehru cried Unity. And in the blazing sunhine a wild, naked man cries in Arabic 'Un Al Huq, Un Al Huq, I am the truth, I am God'. For me holiness was the gratitude I felt having witnessed such things. Pass by pilgrims, pass by.

MAHA AMMA, THE GREAT MOTHER

Bombay is true to herself. Many things may be said about her, but she has little hypocrisy. All that she is, she shows. Becoming a giant peep-show, almost at times a theatre of the absurd.

Her eastern mystery is unveiled. Her comedy and tragedy are shared with all those who care to wander her streets.

She wears a see-through mask. Her beauty is perhaps skin deep. Her philosophy as burning to the mind as the sun that strikes the body.

Beneath that monster sun, friends and foes, tourists and sailors, the masses, drift across her re-claimed body and suck her juices.

The Great Mother greets us all with a 'salaam sahib or ji namaste, go with God, or Bhai, dear brother we are the same - 'Here for so short a while under the eyes of Vishnu, so let us live and work beneath the eyes of our gods who wait in the everlasting halls of eternity to bend our Wills to theirs, now and forever.'

From Vasanta, which is spring, to Shishira, which is the cold season, the truth of the city touches the swaying palm-trees.

Brahmin, Jains, Muslims, Christians, Parsis, Sikhs, Anglo Indians, Pathans and Tribal people, come and go, gaze and wander, suffer and starve. The Land of Nod is their heritage.

Land of kohl and sitar. Of temple scenes strange and disturbing. Of non-violence and of sacrifice.

Bombay shows it all. The licentious gods tall and adored are lazy and ignore the poor, but do not forbid them to be seen. The sick and maimed huddle in doorways of shops. Some of the shops belonging to the jewellers, craftsmen of genius. At least 3,000 of them work in the city offering exotic gems and gold and silver to the rich, who invest large sums of money in all kinds of jewels.

Nothing is hidden away. Along reeking streets, where spiced meat is cooking and then bought wrapped in banana leaves is the honesty of the East. No one is locked up in institutions, the mad and the naked share the pavements with all kinds of incurables. The streets of India are not tidy places for a shopping trip to a hygienic supermarket. No, the streets of the Great Mother are alive with human beings in every act of joy and torment from birth to death. Bombay takes it all into herself and tells the visitor, 'take me as I am and sometimes pity me for the burden of flesh is heavy'.

Once more the fishing dhows with bright red sails dot the Arabian Sea like sea-flowering poinsettias.

No hypocrisy, no answers to old riddles. Only prohibit cow-slaughter posters and an effigy of an ugly giant god being dragged through the streets as the people celebrate the festival of Dashehra.

Once more the balloon wallah cries, 'Come buy, come buy', to the children and the poor dance The Lila, their dance of existence. Who knows, in the painful cycle of metempsychosis they may become the hind leg of a donkey. So in this life they dare not question the gods.

Dharma is duty. Duty is respectable. Hindus have no individuality. The man or woman who does his or her own thing slips off the yoke of Caste and either ends in an opium den or is considered a comic eccentric. At the other extreme he is deified a great saint, a glorious Gandhi.

Tomorrow is another day. It stretches out like its promise. Eat warm pulses and watch the volcanic sunsets burn scarlet into purple into black.

We are all simple little pots made by the potter. We too shatter and break. The All Saints Sisters watch Catholic Goan schoolgirls lighting candles in their chapel. The prayers are for the city. The girls with long plaits and white frocks bend their knees and ask for mercy.

THE BLESSINGS OF KRISHNA

Of all the races that walk the Great Mother's streets, the soul-brothers of Western India are the Gujaratis and the Mahrattas. The Gujaratis are a peace loving dairy farming and trading people. The Mahrattas are tough hill farmers with a militant history. They are horsemen and warriors of Sivaji fame.

Bombay is a power-house of big business, textile mills and factories. Bringing, like the Industrial Revolution did all over the world peasants from the land into towns and factory bench or floor.

The fine silk veil of Indian contradiction is wound around her socialism and idealism. Outrageous capitalism is the question-mark that hangs like a sword over the workers heads. Gone is the Mahratta warrior. Gone is the Gujarati saint.

Nehru was a left-winged Fabian and a total autocrat. Family controlled empires own the major industries. Nationalisation seems a mere puppet idea, as the wealthy élite look down on this weird paradox, from their pent-house apartments at the top of skyscrapers, which they also own. Privilege can be bought with a bribe and the mystery of socialism thickens into a shocking low standard of scandal and corruption.

It is poignant to watch factory workers more used to village life queuing in a decrepit factory dispensary to see the local charity doctor. A line of dejected under-fed men shuffle along waiting their turn. Their faces and their coughs reflect the monotony of their lives. On the walls of the dispensary hang faded posters of Lord Krishna and the dancing elephant god Ganesa both worshipped to bring good fortune and blessings. Also birth-control posters painted in sign language, along with 'Don't spit it is dirty and un-healthy'.

The workers respect the doctor, although brought up on simple Hindu village cures mainly of homeopathic origins. Their teachings tell them of the doctor of the gods Dhan-vantari, who was the inventor of the Ayer-Vedic system of medicine. The god holds in his hands the cup, which contains the liquid of immortality. Like the gods, if a man drinks the ambrosia he will regain his vigour. The workers take their medicine bottles and retreat back to the factory bench as black smoke adds even more heat to the tropical day.

Krishna is a most human god. He is full of life and some-times malice. It is as if he has drained the burning plains of their strength and taken the energy of the land into himself.

The charity hospitals are run like bazaars. Whole families squat around the sick and dying, endlessly rubbing their hands up and down the legs of some pathetic patient. Thin bodies lie, like cardboard cut-outs on mattresses on the floor. Cockroaches and bugs creep around the feet of the dying. The charity doctors and nurses bring an essence of love to those branded with the mark of pain and low-birth. But to the twisted bodies whose limbs are covered with sores and amid the feeble talk of the dying, Lord Krishna will give liberation, for he is a most approachable god! All receive his blessings. All will be delivered from their death-beds and last earthly torment.

Outside a bank of wild orchids are growing. So soon the sun will fade the petals and the green leaves will fall to the ground. And in the morning bright orange marigolds will cover the corpses and an even brighter flame will take its spirit to receive the blessing of Krishna.

VIVASVAT. THE RISING SUN

The Aryan invaders of India came from the North West between 3000 and 1500 B.C. They settled at first in the Punjab the upper valley of the Indus. Where they came into contact with the dark skinned Dravidians, whose culture may be related to the Chaldeans.

While still infatuated with their fair skins the Aryan invaders suppressed the dark skinned race into what is now called Caste. Where everyone has his place and his life-style is bound to his Dharma.

Fatalism pervades the Indian's life from his beginning to his end. He is a tool used by his gods for their satisfaction.

The complex Indian society that so baffles outsiders with its mind-blowing Hinduism came directly from these two races, being added to by tribal peoples who remain untamed and outside of Caste.

In India everything is said to change while everything endures. And all these elements exist side by side; separate yet intermingled.

Indian religions are as complex as the people and those who choose to wander in the everlasting maze of Hinduism should be strong minded as it has been known to cause insanity. The explorer walks an inextricable pathway of exotic legends that lend themselves to the divine. The peasants simplicity of faith is far removed from the Hindu self-disciplines of Ashrams, Jogis, Saints and Philosophers.

The gods known as 'Devas' and the demons as 'Asuras' demand and receive total obeisance. Effigies of devas are sprinkled and perfumed with holy water and piety is shown to she-ogres, female monsters who symbolise the fecundity of nature and the male is worshipped through the symbol of the phallus.

Through the everlasting maze of births and re-births, first, second and third incarnations, superstitions, and avatars of Vishnu, glints a fragment of oriental light. The climate of India rules the people. Their lives go round the fear and glory of their tropical environment. They are nature's children who practice nature-cures and believe in non-violence and vegetarianism. The spotted deer to them is as sacred as the forests he skips in. The gods and goddesses are nature personified. Yama, the judge of men is king of the invisible world. He was born from Vivasvat the sun, that almighty flame in the tropic sky that beats down for months of a year. Baking the earth till it is hard like over-baked bread. And nothing can be planted and nothing can grow. The people have a genetic love of this cruel earth and this flame in the sky. They give their adoration to Indra the rain god who brings the monsoon.

A failed monsoon means famine and death. A flooded river also means death to thousands. So the river-gods are appeased and somewhere between starvation and floods, a people honour the symbols of their religion as an outward sign of an inner devotion. To mother-nature, mother-earth, mother India.

The sun and the storm rule the lives of these agricultural peoples living in the thousands of scattered villages of rural India. Yama who brings death and was the first man ever to die is also called Kala - the weather. The relentless climate rules. The priestly Brahmims and the warriors all bend their knees in prayer to the gods of day and night, fire and water. The spirit that breathes from the flame of the rising sun is Existence and the voices of the gods are heard when the rains crash upon the hard earth.

I am sure that somewhere in the Hindu Pantheon there is a giant octopus with a thousand arms. Each arm, which is a squirming tentacle holds the mystery of Indian thinking within its grasp. And from the churning sea that gave this monster power, he sucks the juices of the climate and with one human eye he stares into the soul of the universe. And as the children of nature try to leap from his grasping arms he bends their Will to face the torments of the burning sky and they obey his order and fall down before Vivasvat-the rising sun.

ELUSIVE HINDUSTAN

'May we keep them, mummy, may we keep them?'
'Keep what darling?'
'The chickens in the bathroom.'
'THE CHICKENS IN THE BATHROOM!'
I went to the servants shower-room, where a pair of cluck-ing hens were trying their best to turn the white tiles into a farm-yard. The new cook had been asked to make us a chicken curry, but I had forgotten to tell him I did not allow the cooks to bring live chickens home. All poultry is sold alive in the markets. In the country bungalow it would have happened without a fuss, but in a Bombay apartment our chicken curry turned into a hectic experience. My children became instant vegetarians. Happy wouldn't stop barking. All his retriever instinct came to life as he waited with drip-ping tongue to hold at least one of the brown hens in his soft mouth.

The 'phone began ringing and all the servants were talking away in their own dialects thinking the whole thing very funny.

I lost my temper with the cook and told him he'd never be able to live in a block of flats. A few days before the chickens I'd found him sitting over a little brazier and smoking fish on the balcony. The fish was delicious, but the apartment smelled like a fishing village and he might have burned the building down. The kitchen was overrun with cockroaches, because he wouldn't use insect spray and he wanted to bring lizards in to catch the cockroaches instead. I had a pale vision of our home being turned into a jungle-hut and decided no matter how hot I became or even if meals were late the cook had to leave and I would cook myself. My houseboy gave me a lesson every morning in kitchen Mahratti and I soon learnt the names of all the vegetables and with his help my coconut based vegetable curry was good enough, even for a Brahmin to eat and the kitchen was scrupulously clean with not one cockroach hiding in a crack on a shelf.

My next door neighbours were a progressive Hindu couple of newly-weds who would not settle for the joint-Hindu living style and bought their own flat. I talked to the wife quite often and I felt even though she did not live in a shared joint-household the household came to her just the same. There was for her no escape and no privacy. All relatives from both sides of the family were in and out of the lift leading to her front door as regularly as the sun blazed and the moon shone. Her younger sister had fallen in love with a Muslim. A more terrible scandal could not have been imagined in a Hindu family! Her brother-in-law had threatened to commit suicide, because he was in the clutches of a money-lender and was about to be ruined. Suicide is a word Hindus cannot come to terms with, because it means someone is making a decision for themselves without their Caste or their plan of destiny coming into it, and this is unthinkable.

The poor new wife could hardly cope with all these problems. No one seemed to bring her good news. She would rock to and fro on her balcony swing rubbing her forehead with ice and I thought in a few years she would be an overweight matron from eating too much white rice and curds along with vegetables fried in oily ghi. She would get too little exercise, her accounts would be added up to the last nai-paise, she would wear her household keys on a belt tied beneath her sari. Next to her husband or even perhaps before him, the king in her life was the rupee, especially in Bombay, which is a money-mad city.

An American lady working for Moral-Rearmament rented another flat in the block and she would come and have long energetic talks about India. I noticed with a smile how she kept washing her hands and that she was about to change the world starting with India first. 'I guess this is the real thing,' she'd say, talking about the Fair Bay. 'This is really India!' Nothing could have been further from the truth. The 'real Hindustan' is as elusive as real love. You may catch glimpses of her as you travel into her villages, live in her cities and wander by her river-banks. Her sky will cover you like a warm, blue blanket and slowly, so slowly with a tread of the tortoise, you will notice that things happen and change and somehow become finished projects. But it's all hard to believe. For Time is given no special meaning and hurry has no special blessings.

Bombay is as far from being the 'real India' as Kerala and its Communism is, or the great wild deserts of Central India or Buddhism or Jainism or endless Castes and Sub-Castes and Sects and wondrous Kashmir. From her purity to her filth, from the Brahmins to the Untouchables and on even to humans, so debased they have to ring bells to let the high born Hindus know they are coming. The outcasts of humanity, but no more the 'real India' than the Saddhus or Muslim Fakirs.

From the Himalayas to a sea-front hotel in Goa, India will play her tricks on your mind and each time you think you have captured the truth it will be blown with the wind or bending with the swaying palms. The palms alone remain defiant against all comers and seekers after the spirit of India. They hold themselves high to greet the ever burning sun and bend themselves low with monsoon winds, but they never break. The secret of Hindustan is in their juice.

India is not for the bigot. Compassion is needed to come to terms with her individual nature. To many she is a dirty, insalubrious scrawl of land called the Sub-Continent. But traveller imbibe her atmosphere of races and seasons, her generosity, her peculiarities, which are extreme, her traditions and her utterances and endeavours and she will drape herself around you like a piece of handwoven cloth and you will become her handmaiden.

For me India is often a word used as a euphemism for survival. The Kathakali dancers move to a dance-discipline ordered from childhood and others from childhood dance through the rubbish tips for their daily bread.

'Memsahib, do not blow out the candle'. How impossible that would be to blow out the candle that is India. Elusive Great Mother burning like an everlasting candle before the high altar of a great and glorious God.

Another Christmas was with us and from my cracker fell a

small plastic pen. An augury without a doubt. Time soon for me to follow my own Dharma. To trace the paths of my own discipline and return to England to write the books that would come at the end of the long preparations a writer has to endure.

The Russian diplomat and his family were also leaving. I invited them in for a Christmas brandy. 'Thank you, no, we Russians do not celebrate Christmas.'

'Oh, what a pity it is such a lovely feast.'

The American lady came instead armed with maps. 'Did you know India is not India on the map, it's how da ya say it 'Bharat'. My husband explained to her that it was from the Sanskrit and may have been the name of the first founder of the Indo-Aryan people. Hindustan was the Muslim name and India was very British. She was now off to the Punjab and I envied her just a little. For the thrill of seeing it all for the first time.

India gliding and fading as the train pulls you along away from the confusion of crowds in the Fair Bay. They melt and vanish, as the train moves into the great silence of red-soil and too blue sky, broken by thousands of crows cawing away as the noise of the train wakes up everything that creeps and crawls and runs. Ah! When the experience crystallized and the crystals were shattered, behold the patterns of a kaleido-scope.

The Hindu lady's brother-in-law had gone off to become a renunciate. He had found the business hounds of Bombay too much for his tender soul. The money-lender was chasing after him. The self-realisation would change both of them.

Pop-groups were coming from the West to sit at the feet of their Gurus and Bombay had television for the first time. A strange meeting of East and West. The big hotels were crowded with foreigners and on the streets of cities like Calcutta, Mother Teresa and her sisters were collecting the dying, the downtrodden and the deserted. 'Balak waited for the curse to be pronounced by Balaam. But instead of cursing them Balaam blessed the people'. The story from the book of Numbers has a profound meaning. No one can become inured to poverty and suffering. The gods and the Castes seem a futile waste of commonsense. There is so much to throw stones at the way novelists and journalists may throw stones. But the poet will bless and the stars will shine down upon the blessed and fresh grass will feed the cattle and giant moths will fly towards the moonlight and their wings will hold small holy pictures of a vibrant land. And the Arabian sea will bring in the fishing boats and the fishermen will bless their catch the way fishermen always blessed the food of the sea and the critics will be lost for words.

e

THE KISS THAT SHOOK THE WORLD

There's a saying that anywhere an Englishwoman goes in the world she will make a garden grow. In the warm seclusion of Malabar Hill the bungalow garden of my English friends always reminded me of home.

The roses had a deeper fragrance than those the flower-seller sold and rhododendrons seemed to ripple with purple and pink lights as birds hummed around the stout branches.

It amazed me for the Indian sun is a demon to tender plants and only sun loving exotics thrive. Yet this garden had a cherry tree in full blossom and Ann told me with pride its name was 'Amanogawa' and it came from Kashmir. Such beauties as Lilium Testaceum was throwing up their lily-white satin heads to the blue sky. The latin names were all part of the fun of growing plants in Indian soil. Nearly all the blooms were taken originally from the foothills of the Himalayas and maybe they were meant to thrive in Bombay, but it all looked so English. The watering-cans and flower-pots and always a bunch of something before I left, shaken with care in case of red ants crawling into the car.

'Do you think I'll get these seeds to take out here, my mother sent them out.'

'I don't know, what are they?'

'Pulsatilla Vulgaris.'

'What — anemones! Why didn't you say so?'

I always thought of anemones as being wind-flowers of the woods and didn't think they would grow in the heat of Ann's Malabar version of a small humid patch of Kew Gardens. But I had a bet with myself that on my next visit Pulsatilla Vulgaris would be sharing the flower-beds with a hedge of Bereris and that would be in flower as well!

On her verandah a basket held four new pups and a sleek pampered cat lazed on the lawn. This is unusual in Bombay where the local cats are thin creatures afraid of the monster rats who sometimes eat them. A box of English export biscuits, an air-mail copy of *The Times* and a new *Vogue* magazine lay on a coffee table. I had to pinch myself to remind me I was in Bombay and not Tunbridge-Wells. Only when our small talk tuned into problems about ayahs and heavy-handed bearers was I back in the Fair Bay.

The Americans I met in Bombay were always scared of a cholera epidemic, which now is a scourge of the past. All drinking water and milk is boiled and only coconut water can be safely drunk out of doors. Our American wife came out to join her husband and looking at the awful drive-in to Bombay from Santa Cruz airport, which is a long, desolate stretch of shanty town dwellings with wild pigs and goats running loose, ordered the driver to take her back to the airport, where she waited for the next plane out. Bombay, India was not for her. No Sir, no way, as the Americans say.

But the unknown American wife was not the centre of the universe and the Fair Bay went on its way without her. The wild pigs grunted in the palm-tree groves and the goats bleated and rubbed their horns against each others backs.

The chaukidar or caretaker at my block of flats stopped me one evening and without a please or thank-you for Hindi has no please or thank-you, asked me in his poor English to give his cousin English lessons. 'Memsahib you will take my paternal cousin and talk with him in your good-enough English for one hour every day coming. Then he will be much improved in English and make a very good scholarship.' To his way of thinking the block of flats was just an extension of joint-family life and he had every right to ask me to teach his cousin. But I knew teaching his cousin to say 'how now brown cow' would most likely cause a cow-riot on the lawns going down to the sea front.

I was being taken to my first Gujerati play. I could not understand a word but enjoyed having the speeches explained to me. The theatre was not air-conditioned and huge fans broke up the heat with bursts of fresh air, above our heads.

The play was pure Hindu mythology for me, but to a devout Hindu I suppose it was a religious offering. The goddess Parvati suffered loneliness and despair, because her husband and god-king Lord Siva had become indifferent to her. She did not have 'another woman' problem, but was weary with her husband's asceticism and contemplations. She turned away from worldly desires and became a hermit. Soon however in the way of the male Siva realised how much he loved and missed his wife. While he was meditating on a sacred mountain-side he saw with his third eye Parvati's beautiful body perfumed and unveiled and ready for love. He turned himself into a young Brahmin and went to visit her. He praised her devotions as a hermit, but asked her to return to the world. The goddess always famed for her temper became angry with the young Brahmin. Without her husband the world did not exist for her. He then revealed himself as Lord Siva her lord and master and husband of a goddess.

After making the usual demands upon him, that women do, when they know they have their man, she agreed to return to the world.

In the tradition of the most ardent gods, Siva took his wife and queen to Mount Kailasa and at last yielded to her with the passion of the heavens.

As they came together their kiss shook the world and it trembled as if on the brink of a mighty earthquake.

As Parvati slept in her husband's arms the embrace became the quiet moment of perfect sleep and the lakes of the world were calm and the heavens were calm and a deep peace held the forests almost in a trance as one by one the animals lay down to rest.

THE DAWN

A dawn breeze blew into my bedroom. The mosquito-net gently moved into thin white folds as the breeze lifted the ends of it from the marble floor. My family were sleeping. Morning was still a few hours away, soon the apartment would echo with the beginning daytime sounds. The servants would wake and have their showers. Our ayah would oil her hair, comb it into a thick bun then put on a spotless white cotton sari. The houseboy would wear a pair of morning shorts and a clean bush-shirt and the sweeper woman would come in a faded blue or purple homespun sari tied above her knees so she could wash the floors without getting it wet.

I opened the side of the mosquito-net, open windows framed the sea and palms like a water-colour waiting to be hung. During the day the sea gleamed brilliant blue. In early dawn I could smell the salt air and a mist as close fitting as the nets around the bed shrouded the sea from sight.

Ushas, the dawn goddess was waking the city. Vedic poets sing her special hymns because she brings the sleeping world to action and movement. Fire is her lover and she is the mother of the sun. In her chariot of early sunlight pulled along by holy cows she sends the night away and brings light to the world. She gives the birds their songs and tiny babies wake for their early morning feed. She likes to let the wicked sleep and wake only the good. Her plans alas go astray at times and the power of her charms wakes saints and sinners. They stir and leave their dreams behind as Ushas immortal goddess touches the forest creatures on their soft bellies and they wake hungry for food.

In the apartment directly underneath ours, a family of Sindhis kept a talking parrot. In the first light of morning this chatterbox could be heard talking away with the dawn chorus of Bombay crows, shouting in a boozy voice 'bring ripe ones' in Hindi. The odd fantasy of servants bringing 'ripe ones' made me laugh. The Sindhis are Hindu refugees from Pakistan, who left after Partition. They are considerable business people, but rather gaudy in their tastes. Their homes are reflections of their shops, every ornament imaginable is on show along with cheap plastic idols, garlands of mari-golds and the heavy smell of Indian scent. The dawn now had complete control of the sky. First light made me restless and I watched the stars leave a stencil outline against the pale blue vapour. Soon our ayah would bring in a tray of orange-flavoured tea. Then I'd toss pancakes sprinkled with lemon juice for my husband. He'd read the Indian Times before leaving for the High Court. Mary would take my daughter to school and my son would go for a morning play on the beach with Happy before the sun was up.

Then one after another the people I called my morning-wallahs would call. The dhobi to collect the dirty washing. The butcher with fresh cuts of meat and the greengrocer would squat outside the front door as Mary fussed over the vegetables. Already the servants were boiling their rice for the day and the first deep heat began to filter through the air making everyone yawn.

A string of flies would follow the fisherwoman down the back stairs and out into the street. We could have lived six flights up forever without having to go out for shopping. The tailor brought a new dress, even a Kashmiri salesman came and spread rugs and cotton bedspreads all over the marble floor telling me all the needlework was embroidered by the men in Kashmir. He asked me hundreds of rupees for a rug and I'd bate him down, till we were both exhausted from the deal and needed glasses of lime-juice before bargaining could begin again.

By mid-afternoon when the housewives were sleeping a noisy group of left-wing students were chanting rebellious themes in the square below. A speck of red flag could be seen between the palms. Was this a positive omen for Bombay.

India is like a strong horse it throws most of its riders up to the sky for the gods to play with. To stay the course the horseman must be pretty good, but was the horse becoming weak?

Charity nuns would knock for alms and friends drop in. Often we would go for a morning breakfast picnic thirty miles or more from the Fair Bay and be back before the sun shrivelled our enthusiasm.

Ushas pays her morning respect to the sun the king of the heavens. The bearer is going to market and I ask him if Sahib gave him enough money. 'Kuchh rupaya hai?' He gives me a toothy grin and together we go through the shopping list. He will take his time. Browsing in the markets, gossiping about us the family he works for with other servants. Smoking an evil looking weed made from cow-dung. He'll come home full of it all, like an excited boy. Telling us he's seen some tribal women of the Coorgi tribe from the South and not often seen in Bombay. The attraction is their bare breasts. They wear a sari but no choli the thin sari-blouse and their naked backs and breasts peep surreptitiously through the sari-drape. Causing a mild sensation on the Bombay streets.

The day gradually reached its peak like the climax of Indian classical ragas. The tormenting music played by Muslim sitar players who strum the strings into a tone-orgasm and the mind is released instead of the body. The day then burned itself into a hot night and charismatic Christians brought holy dancing filled with the Holy Spirit to Bombay. Praising The Lord and shaking hands with those who were saved.

At midnight I kiss my sleeping children and see there are no insects in their bedrooms. Give our dog a bowl of iced water and sit for awhile on the balcony thinking about the day.

The chatterbox parrot is still giving orders in Hindi. On my dressing-table are a handful of green leaves given to me at a Muslim festival. 'Memsahib they will turn to gold, after one year, you wait.' Ushas dawn goddess since the world began turns the Indian day to gold. Preparing the way for the golden sun-flowers, opening their golden petals. Women wear dozens of golden bangles, gold sandals cover their feet. Golden threads spangle their saris, the children have gold glints in their eyes and birds show off golden plumes. The Great Mother sometimes shows us her golden heart. The wheat is gold and the sea is like warm gold when worn near living flesh.

O sister of night, mother of the sun, ever re-born young and fresh, wake the sleeping city and let your golden promise of a new day rise and fall as the temple bells peal out notes to honour Ushas — the dawn.

HOLI, FORGIVING AND BEGINNING

Before the long arms of Hindu traditions and the spirit of Hindu mythology, enslave my mind and I become re-absorbed into the culture, I shall leave the Fair Bay.

Before India changes me as it always changes the traveller for better or worse, I shall leave the pagan splendour for others to discover. The seasons have tossed the Great Mother hither and thither. From spring to winter she has unfolded herself.

City of marigolds, city of sunsets, of servants gossip and annual rains. Of pan eating and betel nut spitting peoples. Of red tongues and ugly old teeth. City of eastern enlightenment the reward of perfect knowledge after a lifetime search for Brahma, perfect beyond all the gods of the world. City of Atma, the universal soul, the all in which we live and move and have our beings. City of sandal-paste for painting decorations on walls and stairs to give greetings at births and weddings and feasts of simple joy. Bombay of the banyan trees. Of re-claimed muddy islands, of funeral pyres and glossy, expensive hotels.

City of Hindus in dhotis and Muslims in pyjamas. Of Parsis who are fair and Dravidians who are black. Of Jains who so honour life they shake a grass-whisk in front of them as they walk, so no insect will be harmed. City of Ben-Israel Jews and Pathans who trace their line back to Alexander The Great. They are loyal tribal men who would lay their lives down for a friend.

City of banks and businesses of enormous wealth, and iced coffee on hot mornings with special friends. Of fickle, lovely filmstars as beautiful as the giant butterflies that flutter in and out of the tropic flowers. Richman, beggar-man and thief walk the hot pavements together as water-melons burst their seeds.

I wonder at it all. The way India causes wonder and pain. Looking at the tourists who hope to see a chaste Hindu widow committing suttee,* but on being told the law forbids it now, will settle for a daytime trip to Aarey the milk-colony to eat ice-cream and drink milk-shakes made from rich buffalo milk. Or they go off to Borivili to pay their respects to the Gandhi Memorial. Then, I see young travellers from Europe looking for the distant, impossible dream sung by Vedic poets. The hospitality of a kind people who are childish in their curiosity, yet will reach a point of hysteria in their wild mystic festivals, that usually disgust Europeans.

The Great Mother holds them together. These dependent, helpless, responsive people who walk her streets and praise her gods. Who is the deceived, where is the deceiver? Quest-ions linger on a lotus leaf and answers are lost at the tip of a green parrots beak.

Hundreds are walking towards a fair. The fair-ground is worn-out looking and the noise ear-splitting. The people are buying organs of the body made of clay and then taken into the temples to be prayed over, so that anyone suffering with a sickness of those parts may be cured.

Indian music beats out a wail of despair as pickpockets steal and the fair-ground wheel goes round and round.

The night shows up trees lit with fairy-lights as a rich Parsi family hold a reception in the grounds of the Willingdon Club. The air is thick with Indian perfumes and jewels shim-mer. Young film-actresses arrive draped in saris that have cost hundreds of rupees. All the social butterflies drift around the Indian film director giving the party. Amid the gossip, reputations are made and lost and love affairs begun and ended. Buffet meals are taken off banana leaves and a Sheik may be seen giving the eye to a pretty sari-clad girl he wants for his harem. For his favourite wife he may want to buy Marine Drive and The Queen's Necklace.

To the American guests nothing is hygienic and the Eng-lish girls look awful dressed-up in saris, because they don't go with blonde hair. They all dance to music from a Goan

*Suttee — Rite of widow throwing herself in the flames with dead husband

band till the reception ends. The tree lights are dimmed, the cars speed into the coming dawn and the cleaning up is left to servants. The moon sheds an indifferent shadow over the atmosphere left by the rich idlers and soon it will be another day.

The Fair Bay will once again awake to the Cries of India, as the people take their places in the order of their Dharma, which has been thrust upon their shoulders till the end of Time.

I feel drained. India has overwhelmed my emotions. I will go away only to return. I know I shall need to return if only to search for that part of myself that wanders in the old streets and villages. The East does not allow her image to be broken. It remains a puzzle, a quest, a torment beneath a burning sun.

Christ said, 'The poor are always with us'. Will there be another golden age for India, where want and suffering rot in a distant haze. Where ignorance from rich and poor, educated and illiterate is done to death. Ah, gods are you still with me on our journey through the city of sandals? Can you hear the Great Mother singing her song of life? Will you release them all from their re-births, and let them find oblivion? Will jogis perform a feat of super-human power and with their soothsaying save this city from herself?

And when I return to listen to Sikh jokes and eat curry with my hands, to see cacti-fences around the flat, difficult fields, where the stubborn earth is hardbaked and red. To see thousands of small babies with huge black eyes. To see brass everywhere and listen to temple bells. To hear a woman scream in labour and watch an old man dying. To gaze up at a heaven filled with stars brighter than diamonds, and listen to the waves tossing against the rocks on Indian beaches.

I remember I was meant to be a traveller. But views sometimes bored me and strange customs and the political stench from new governments got on my nerves. Crowds of flesh undernourished, idol worshipping and afraid caught my attention every day. I swayed mentally half with pity, half with disgust. Always with anger for humanities sake.

Smallpoxed peasants chewed superstition. Worshipped Krishna on their knees, which were thin and cracked like their backs, covered with dirty cotton. Children hungry and deformed were left to Hindu idols by sad mothers who sit ringing handfuls of golden bells to wake licentious gods who always sleep. Tall, well-nourished gods ignore the poor.

When the sweat of a Bombay bazaar is a memory of coloured bangles, silks, black-oiled hair and painted sandals and nagging beggars, within myself I shall carry seas and people. Hills of tropical flowers, skies mounted with rainbows. A moon I'd like to see again and great downpours of rain and silly flies. Strange, spicy food and wet, sticky fruits and peasants scratching lice.

When they have all gone. The peasants, the sun, into their own sweet prisons, I should have left my footsteps on their huge beaches. But sand moves with the sea, leaving only patterns for tiny crabs to scuttle over.

I shall return to my own world. We all do in the end. No one mothers the weary tribes who lend their hearts to discovery in overcrowded lands.

Tremendous doubts astonish me. As I trespass my step is my desire. I want to denounce so much, yet useless statements lighten nothing. So, for awhile let the birds sing. The Great Mother will be here when I come back and I shall be glad.

It is the festival of Holi*. The people are running in the streets throwing bright red paint over each other and every passer-by gets splashed. Holi — it is all over, forgiving and beginning.

When I was an announcer with All India Radio I used to end the evening transmission by saying, 'This is All India Radio wishing all our listeners goodnight and Jai Hind.' And so, goodnight Bombay City Of Sandals and Goodbye.

Jai Hind, forever India.

*Holi — Spring Festival

INDEX and GLOSSARY

107 **AVATAR** –
Hindu reincarnation of godhead.

15 **AYAH** –
Hindu nannie. *No! Any religion – usually Catholic.*

105 **AYER VEDIC** –
Of Aryan beginnings – Hinduism.

121 **ATMA** –
The Universal Soul – Hinduism.

(B)

112 **BALAAM** –
The O.T. Book of Numbers.

112 **BALAK** –
The O.T. Book of Numbers.

57 **BALLARD PIER** –
Landing Stage at Bombay Harbour.

11 **BANIA** –
Hindu Money Lender, of the Merchant Caste.

46 **BANDRA** –
Bombay suburb.

12 **BANYAN** –
Fig-bearing tree.

84 **BAPUJI** –
Affectionate Hindu name for Gandhi.

98 **BARA SAHIB** –
Raj – 'Sir' or 'Master'. *Not necessarily Raj.*

37 **BAS** –
Enough! (Hindi).

100 **BENARES** –
Indian city of temples and silk-making.

102 **BHAI** –
Brother (Hindi).

15 **BLACK SACRED THREAD** –
Worn by Brahmin children (Hindus). *All ages.*

88 **BLUE VALLEY (THE)** –
Hill Station Valley.

122 **BORIVILI** –
Gandhi's Shrine.

11   BRAHMA –
Hindu Godhead.

(C)

32   CASTE –
Social Hindu Order of Class.

42   CAVES OF ELEPHANTS –
Caves near Bombay.

99   CHAPATTI –
Indian flat bread.

54   CHAPPLES –
Indian sandals.

98   CHOTA SAHIB –
Raj – small, not very important master – Hindu.   *N.N.R.*

37   CHAUPATI –
Beach in Bombay.

88   CONNAUGHT RIDE (THE) –
Hill Station.

27   CRAWFORD MARKET –   *Much more than fruit + veg.*
Fruit and Vegetable market in Bombay.

(D)

106   DEVAS –
Hindu Gods.

32   DHAL –   *Any pulses.*
Lentils.

105   DHANVATARI –
Hindu God of Medicine.

33   DHARMA –
Duty.

79   DHOBI –
Laundry washerman – Hindu.

89   DHOBI WATERFALLS –
Hill Station.

15   DHOTI –   *?*
Hindu man's trouser drape.

14   DHOWS –   *Not nec. fishing.*
Fishing boat.   *A type of boat indigenous to Arabia.*

103   DASHEHRA –
Hindu festival.

(E)

30   ELLORA –
Caves.

(F)

89   FALLS OF YENA –
Hill Station.

(G)

85   GANESA or GANESH –
Hindu Elephant God.
43   GATEWAY OF INDIA –
Archway leading from Harbour.
42   GHI –   No. – Coconut, mustard oils + others.
Clarified butter used for all Indian cooking.
9   GREAT MOTHER –
Bombay.
70   GREAT THAR –
Indian Desert.
78   GRISHMAR –
The Hot Season.
23   GOAN – No! Goans are 55% Hindu.
Indian Catholic from ex-Portuguese Goa.
31   GUJARAT –
Western Indian State (Bombay).
23   GUJARATI – No! Marathi 1st. – Gujarati 2nd.
Language spoken by most Hindus in Bombay.

(H)

37   HANGING GARDENS –
Pleasure-Gardens, Bombay.
93   HEMANTA –
Winter season (Hindi).

68 HINDI –
Official language of India.
69 HIRANYAGARBHA –
Legend of the Golden Egg (Hindu Mythology).
124 HOLI –
Spring Festival.
88 HUNTER'S POINT –
Hill Station.
98 HYSON –
Chinese Green Tea.

(I)

81 IMAM – *No!. No priests in Islam. Prayerwallah r Muezzin.*
Muslim Priest.
67 INDRA –
Hindu God.
35 ISMAILIA –
The Red Sea.

(J)

124 'JAI HIND' –
Victory to India or Forever India (Hindi).
102 JAINS –
Sect of Hindus.
37 'JALDI KAO' –
'Make haste!' 'Make haste!' (Hindi).
102 'JI NAMASTE' –
'Go with God'. (Hindi).
23 JOGI –
Hindu Mystic.
44 JUHU –
A beach.

(K)

107 KALA –
The weather.

69   KALI MA –
The black mother –Hindu demon goddess.
42   KARLI –
Cave outside Bombay.
13   KARTIK –
Month of October – New Moon.
111   KATHAKALI –
Indian Classical Dancing.
111   KERALA –
Southwestern Indian State.
15   KHADDI –
Hand-woven cloth.
30   KHALSA –
Purity of Faith – the Sikhs.
23   KHANA –
Dinner.
32   KHOL –
Black cosmetic powder brushed on eyelids.
33   KONKAN COAST –
Bombay coastline.
81   KORAN –
Muslim Holy Book.
10   KRISHNA –
(Lord) – Hindu God.
88   KRISHNA VALLEY –
Hill Station.
119   'KUCHH RUPAYA HAI?' –
'Have you got enough money?' (Hindi).

(L)

41   LAKH –
100,000 rupees.
13   LAKSHMI –
Hindu goddess.
102   LAND OF NOD –
India.
99   'LE JAO' –
'Try this.' (Hindi).

54   LILA (THE) —
Dance of Existence (Hindu).
42   LINGHAM —
Phallic.

(M)

23   MADU —
Hindu male name.
88   MAHABALESHWAR —
Hill Station.
42   MAHALAKSHMI —
Hindu Temple in Bombay.
9   MAHA AMMA —
The Great Mother (Hindi).
92   MAH JONGG —
Chinese game.
29   MAHRATTA —
People of Muharashtra.
82   MALABAR HILL —
Exclusive Residential area in Bombay.
55   MALI —
Gardener.
28   MANGO —
Tropical fruit.
37   MARATHI —
Indian Language.
24   MATHERAN —
Hill Station
68   MAYA —
Illusion (Hindi).
81   MECCA —
Muslim city of pilgrimage in the Middle East.
28   MEMSAHIB —
Raj — Miss or Mrs.   N.N.R.
70   MOKSHA —
Heaven (Buddhist).
12   MONSOON —
Seasonal winds that bring rains.

82   MOSQUE –
Muslim Church   *Really!!!*

97   MAHARASHTRA –
State of Bombay.

27   MULLA –
Muslim priest.   *No!*

11   MUMBAI –
Bombay (vernacular).

36   MUSSULMAN –
Muslim.

(N)

73   NAGAS –
Snake demons (Hindu).

73   NAGINA –
Female Snake demon.

66   NAI PAISE –
1/100th of a rupee.

82   NARAKA –
Hindu Hell.

70   NIRVANA –
Hindu paradise.

(P)

83   PALLA –
Indian Ocean Fish.

15   PAN –
Betel-nut leaf, chewed after meals.

98   PANI –
Water.

23   PAPAYA –
Tropical melon-like fruit.

81   PARBHATI –
Goddess.

11   PARVATI –
Goddess, wife of Lord Siva.

102   PATHANS –
Tribal men of Afghanistan.

102 PARSI – *No! Zoroastrian!*
Persian.
81 PUJA –
Prayer offering.
81 PURDA – *No!. Purda is the state of female retirement. Not curtains!*
Curtain drape worn by Muslim women (Tent-like).

(Q)

40 QUEEN'S NECKLACE –
Lights along Marine Drive, Bombay.

(R)

119 RAGA –
Traditional form of Hindu music.
30 RAJPUT –
Native of Rajasthan.
81 RAMADAN –
Muslim fast lasting one month.
38 RAVI SHANKAR –
A Musician. A famous Sitar player.
71 RUPEE –
Unit of money.

(S)

24 SANSKRIT –
Classical Indian Language.
10 SARI –
Indian female dress.
73 SESHA –
Snake god (Hindu).
38 SHABASH –
Wonderful.
25 SHARADA –
Autumn.
102 SHISHIRA –
Cold Season.
38 SITAR –
Indian string instrument.
81 SIVA –
Hindu god.

43 SIVAJI –
Indian hero. *Maratha*

51 SRIMATI –
Holy Mother (Mrs).

45 SUTRA –
Hymn.

122 SUTTEE – *Suicide.*
Hindu funeral rite for widows.

64 SWAMIS –
Hindu Holy Men.

(T)

73 TAKSHAKA –
Snake-god King.

68 TAMIL –
South Indian Language.

98 THALI –
Brass dinner plate (Hindu).

38 THORA –
Little.

82 TOWERS OF SILENCE –
Parsi Tombs. *Not Tombs! They are not buried.*

(U)

101 UN AL HUQ – *No!!! Blasphemous in Islam!*
I am God (Arabic).

67 UNTOUCHABLE –
Hindu lowest caste.

64 UPANISHADS –
Hindu holy readings.

95 URDU –
Classical Language.

120 USHAS –
Hindu goddess of the Dawn.

(V)

72 VAISYAS – *No! Sudras are lowest caste.*
The common people (Hindi).

12   VARSHA –
        The rains.
18   VASANTA –
        Spring.
64   VEDIC PRAYERS –
        Hindu.
73   VISHNU –
        Hindu god.
106   VIVASVAT –
        The Sun.

(W)

14   WALLAH –
        Fellow.
88   WESTERN GHATS –
        Range of Hills.

(Y)

107   YAMA –
        The first man (i.e. Adam).

(Z)

24   ZOROASTER –
        Persian Prophet.